"So, what made today such a rough day?" Jessica asked, looking up at him through her lashes as she sipped at her coffee.

Jeremy was so lost in her curious and concerned eyes, he forgot to speak. All he could think of was that she must have stopped by to see him. She wasn't working. She wasn't with friends. So she had to be here to see him. Unreal.

"You know," he answered finally, "suddenly my day doesn't seem so important. But there is something else. . . . I was just wondering . . . There's this party on Friday night, and I thought maybe you'd like to go."

Jessica blinked.

"With me," Jeremy finished uncertainly. Jeremy saw a small smile start to play on Jessica's lips, but it was gone so quickly, he was left wondering if he'd imagined it. The spark in her eyes seemed to fizzle, and she suddenly seemed strangely distant.

*I read her wrong,* Jeremy thought, a sickening feeling seeping into his heart. *She's not remotely interested.*

Don't miss any of the books in SWEET VALLEY HIGH
SENIOR YEAR, an exciting new series from Bantam Books!

*Visit the Official Sweet Valley Web Site on the Internet at:*

**http://www.sweetvalley.com**

Francine Pascal's

# SVH senioryear

# If You Only Knew

## CREATED BY
## FRANCINE PASCAL

BANTAM BOOKS
NEW YORK • TORONTO • LONDON • SYDNEY • AUCKLAND

RL 6, age 12 and up

IF YOU ONLY KNEW

*A Bantam Book / June 1999*

**17th Street Productions**

Produced by 17th Street Productions,
a division of Daniel Weiss Associates, Inc.
33 West 17th Street
New York, NY 10011.

ISBN: 0-553-49279-9

*Published simultaneously in the United States and Canada*

*Bantam Books are published by Bantam Books, a division of Random*
*House, Inc. Its trademark, consisting of the words "Bantam Books" and*
*the portrayal of a rooster, is Registered in U.S. Patent and Trademark*
*Office and in other countries. Marca Registrada. Bantam Books, 1540*
*Broadway, New York, New York 10036.*

PRINTED IN THE UNITED STATES OF AMERICA

OPM     0 9 8 7 6 5 4 3 2 1

*To Noemi Barriga*

# Conner McDermott

Ever hear the expression "damned if you do, damned if you don't"? It's the dilemma of being repulsed by something and attracted to it at the same time.

Like with coffee. People drink it for the taste, the buzz, the sensation of holding a warm mug in their chubby little hands, or even because sipping the stuff makes them feel intellectual. Some people can't even begin their days without it.

But then there's the downside. Caffeine headaches when they don't get enough; yellowed teeth if they drink too much. It's a turn-on and an aggravation all at once.

Sort of like Elizabeth Wakefield.

# Elizabeth Wakefield

If a guy kisses you and then runs away, is that good or bad? It could mean he thinks it was a mistake and wants to forget it ever happened. Then again, maybe he was so blown away by the kiss that he didn't know what else to do. I'm hoping for number two, but Conner is so hard to read that I have no way of knowing. So the next question is, do I ask him about it?

# Jeremy Aames

I've only known Jessica Wakefield for two days, but I can't stop thinking about her. She's intelligent, totally beautiful, and so fun to be with that she actually makes me forget the rest of my life is falling apart—it's like she's so full of energy that it's contagious. But she has a quiet side too. There's something vulnerable about her that makes me want to get to know her even more. I guess the only thing to do is ask her out. Of course, first I have to find her and figure out why she ran off so suddenly this afternoon.

Let's just hope it wasn't because I repulse her.

# Jessica Wakefield

## Sucky Things That Have Happened to Me Lately

1. Lila and Melissa told Jeremy that I'm the slut of SVH. I took off before I actually heard them, but they must have. Restraint isn't exactly one of their strong points.

2. Elizabeth got me fired from Healthy because she decided to be irresponsible for the first time in her perfect existence. She was supposed to work my shift, but she never showed, so now I'm jobless.

3. I talked to Coach Laufeld after the game — she called to let me know she's benching me for the next game. Then she informed me that (surprise!) I'm not

captain of the squad anymore. Not that I expected to be anything after missing the pep rally, but I was still hoping. On the bright side — if you can call it that — Tia was named captain instead of Melissa, which should make things a little more bearable. I hope.

4. It's Saturday night, but instead of having a date (social lepers don't get many offers, you know), I'm stuck at the Fowlers' with nothing to do but watch crappy TV with my parents. I'll probably just end up doing homework, which reminds me:

5. I have a huge project for drama class due next week, and I don't have the slightest clue where to start.

Did I mention that my life sucks?

# CHAPTER
## The Best-Laid Plans

**1**

Will held Melissa close and swayed back and forth. He nuzzled his face into her soft, chestnut brown hair, inhaling the familiar scent of her apple-blossom shampoo with each breath.

"It's going to be okay, you know," Will murmured as he moved his hand in large, slow circles on her back. But even as he said the words, he couldn't help wondering if he was telling the truth. He knew Melissa was going to need some time to recover from this blow. Her heart had been set on being captain of the cheerleading squad. It was all she'd talked about for weeks. And now it was like the earth had fallen out from beneath her feet.

Melissa pulled away and walked over to the car. She boosted herself onto the hood, her arms at her sides and her entire body slumping heavily. She was still wearing her cheerleading uniform, and it somehow made her look even more frail. Slowly she lifted her head to look at him.

"But it's not okay, Will. Don't you see?" Melissa

1

said, her voice little more than a whisper. "This is our senior year. You're first-string quarterback, and I was supposed to be the cheerleading captain, but now I have to sit back while Tia Ramirez runs the squad. Tia," she repeated, her voice trembling. "Tia would never even have been *considered* for captain if we were still at El Carro." She stared at him, the tears welling up again.

Will walked closer, his feet stirring up tiny grains of sand that had found their way onto the paved parking lot. In the moonlight he could see the moistness reflected around Melissa's swollen eyes—the result of nearly two hours of crying. He touched her face gently with his thumb, wiping away a few stray tears. Her skin was as cold as it was pale.

Will took off his new Sweet Valley High football jacket and draped it around her shoulders. Melissa's features softened slightly. She tugged at the jacket's collar, pulling it tightly around herself. Will had seen Melissa this way many times, and he'd always stood by her. That was just part of being her boyfriend. He tried to tell himself that it would be that way in any relationship, but somehow he knew that life with Melissa was more dramatic than it would be with other girls. Over the years he had learned to accept that.

"Are you all right?" he asked.

"I guess," Melissa responded.

She dabbed at her eyes and nose with a tissue she'd pulled from her bag earlier. Then she crumpled it up and put her hands back under her legs. She stared up at Will, her pale blue eyes so large and vulnerable that he wished he could scoop her up and hold her in his arms forever. He wanted to protect her from all of the pain in the world—the pain that always seemed to surround her.

"Thanks for hanging out with me," she said quietly.

Her grateful tone caused a pang in Will's heart, and he was suddenly overcome with guilt. What if he had followed through with his original plan to break up with her tonight? To leave her so that he would be free to date Jessica Wakefield.

Jessica. Beautiful, lighthearted Jessica. He had to push his thoughts of her aside. There was no way he could leave Melissa now. She would never get through this alone. She needed him, and Will liked to be needed.

"I know it's not fair, Liss," he said, putting his arms around her again. "I really do. I know how much you wanted to be captain, and you deserved it. Way more than Tia." He held her close and kissed her head lightly. "Or anyone else," he added as an afterthought, knowing that his dismissal of Jessica would make her feel more secure.

But Melissa wasn't done crying yet. She brought her hands to her face, and her whole body

3

began to shake. Will pulled her even closer, enveloping her in his strong arms and resting his chin on her head.

"Go ahead and cry, Liss," he said quietly, staring at the rough surf in the distance. "I'm here for you, and I'm not going anywhere."

"Hello, Aames? Anyone in there?"

Jeremy Aames started at the sound of a familiar voice. It was Corey Scott, one of his coworkers at House of Java.

"Snap out of it, daydream boy," Corey ordered, with attitude to spare.

"Sorry," Jeremy apologized, turning to face her black-rimmed eyes and dyed black hair. "Did you say something?"

Corey narrowed her eyes. "Only about ten times, but don't worry about it. I'm sure you were thinking about something *really* important—like football."

Jeremy wasn't in the mood for Corey's sarcasm. Unfortunately she had nailed him—he had been thinking about that day's game. He was the captain of Big Mesa High's football team, and he'd just led his squad in a gloryless loss against Sweet Valley High.

Then, instead of joining his friends over a few pizzas to commiserate, he'd had to come to work as usual. It had been a long time since Jeremy had been able to participate in the bonding rituals that took place off the football field. That was just the way it had to be. For now.

Jeremy looked at Corey, who was staring at him with her arms folded across her chest.

"So what exactly did you say?" he asked in as level a tone as he could manage. Corey rolled her eyes and sighed.

"I said I think I can handle this massive crowd for a while if you want to take your break," she offered, gesturing at the nearly empty café.

"Oh, thanks." Jeremy untied the strings on his green apron. He saw Corey start to open her mouth, so he quickly ducked into the back room before she could let another derisive comment fly.

Jeremy threw his apron over a chair and plopped down on the beat-up maroon couch. His manager, Ally Scott, Corey's more normal sister, had finally given in and set up an area in the back room where the staff could hang out or eat during breaks. Of course, she hadn't wanted to spend much money, so the "area" consisted of an old couch, an even older chair, and a table holding a bunch of out-of-date magazines and a Princess phone. The rest of the room was lined with stock shelves and contained another small area with a desk that served as Ally's office.

Jeremy leaned forward and pulled the phone over from the opposite side of the table. He dialed

Jessica Wakefield's number and almost crossed his fingers for luck.

"Don't be mad at me," Jeremy whispered. "Just don't be mad at *me*." Jessica had run off so suddenly when he had seen her earlier that afternoon, he'd spent most of the rest of the day wondering if he'd somehow offended her.

"Hello?"

Jeremy's heart skipped a beat at the sound of a young female voice, but then he realized it was too high-pitched to be Jessica's.

"Hi, this is Jeremy Aames. May I speak with Jessica, please?" he said automatically. Then he grimaced. His friends always teased him for being so polite and formal, but his polished manners had been perfected by several years of country-club butt kissing. Once Jeremy had been the perfect socialite son, but these days he tried to repress that side as much as possible.

"She's not here right now," the voice answered flatly.

"Would you mind telling her I called?" Jeremy asked.

"Yeah, sure. Whatever," she said. Then the line went dead.

*What's her deal?* Jeremy wondered, trying to remember if Jessica's sister, Elizabeth, had ever mentioned another, ruder sister. Nothing came to mind.

6

Jeremy hung up the phone, leaned back into the soft couch cushions, and clasped his hands behind his head. He hadn't been able to find Jessica on the sidelines after the game, so he'd assumed she had gone right home. If that were the case, then where was she?

"Don't be a moron, Aames," he said to himself. "She probably just went out with some friends. She's probably celebrating with the football team right now."

The thought of Jessica surrounded by a bunch of Sweet Valley jocks caused a major pang of jealousy.

Jeremy chewed at his lower lip. He just wanted to know if Jessica was angry at him so he could quit obsessing about it. Because right now there was only one explanation for Jessica's bizarre behavior, and Jeremy didn't like it.

He had a sneaking suspicion Jessica was blowing him off.

"Oh! Get popcorn too, Andy," Tia instructed as Andy Marsden made his way to the concession stand at the movie theater.

"And make it an extra large," Maria added. "I don't want to be picking at the kernels before we even get through the previews."

Andy stopped suddenly and turned to look at Maria.

"Are you kidding me?" he asked, his chin angled down while his eyes stared up at her. "When was the last time you went to the movies?"

Maria was too surprised to respond, which was fine, because Andy didn't give her a chance.

"Are you aware that an extra-large popcorn is roughly the size of an oil drum?" he continued.

Maria laughed. "Hey, there are three of us," she told him. "And besides, from what I hear, Tia can really pack in the popcorn," she added, throwing a mischievous glance in Tia's direction.

"You heard right," Tia responded, nodding and causing her high ponytail to bob up and down. "Last time Angel and I were here, I think I ate an oil drum and a half all by myself." Maria and Tia giggled, but Andy just rolled his eyes in mock exasperation.

"Yeah, but your boyfriend is a pig," Andy said.

"Hey! Watch it!" Tia said.

"Fine, fine," he conceded, holding up his hand, "I'll get what you want. But that means someone's gotta stay out here and help me carry everything in."

"I'll stay," Maria offered, jumping at the chance to remain in the lobby. She wanted to have a clear view of the entrance for a little while longer. "You can go get seats, Tia."

Tia shrugged. "You sure? 'Cause I don't mind waiting for Andy if you want to go in."

"No, that's all right. I'll stay," Maria reaffirmed, tugging at the bottom of her crocheted tank top. "I can keep an eye out for Conner while Andy's on line."

The moment Maria heard her own words, she wanted to take them back. Andy and Tia exchanged one of those "poor, pathetic Maria" looks.

"Why would Conner be here?" Tia inquired, lowering one eyebrow.

"I told him we would be here," Andy explained. "I don't know how Maria knew I told him, though."

Maria blushed. *I was eavesdropping?* she thought. *No need to tell them that.* Of course, she had to tell them something since they were both staring her down.

"It's no big deal, you guys," Maria said. "I just overheard you at the party this afternoon, telling Conner we'd be here, so I thought he might show up." Sure, Conner had been Maria's main reason for coming, but she didn't want Tia and Andy to know that.

"Oh. Well, he did seem really psyched," Andy said. "He's been wanting to see this movie for a long time."

Maria tried not to smile. It sounded like a Conner encounter was a definite.

"I hate to disappoint," Tia said, "but if he's not here yet, he's probably not coming. Conner may

9

be laid-back about a lot of things, but I've never seen him late to a movie. He's really picky about where he sits—something about 'optimal viewing conditions,'" she said, imitating Conner's tone. "And besides, he thinks the previews are the best part."

Maria's heart dropped, but she tried not to let it show. Nothing was less attractive than desperation.

"Oh, that's too bad," she said, as indifferently as she could. "Maybe next time."

Maria was ready to move on to another topic of conversation. She had been having a hard time playing it cool when it came to Conner—ever since he'd heartlessly dumped her, actually. But Tia and Andy weren't quite ready to drop it.

"Hey, at least we won't have to listen to him dissect the whole film when it's over," Tia responded with a slight giggle.

"You mean like that time he insisted that *101 Dalmatians* was Disney's poor attempt at film noir?" Andy said, barely able to stifle his laughter long enough to finish the sentence.

"And then he said that the ending would have been more realistic if Cruella de Vil had just made the damn coat!" Tia's voice cracked as she struggled to get the words out. She put her arm on Andy's shoulders for balance as the two of them nearly doubled over, laughing.

Maria observed their exchange, enjoying the

little Conner anecdotes. Tia and Andy were so lucky. They had a history with Conner. They had grown up with him. Maria kept wishing that she could have that kind of free and easy relationship with him, but with one exception. She wanted to be more than a friend.

"I'd love to hear some of his theories," Maria said. "We'll have to get him to come with us next time."

Tia wiped at the tears in the corners of her eyes and sighed. "Yeah, he's definitely entertaining," she said, breathless from her laugh fest.

"I bet he is," Maria said quietly. Part of her wanted to bag the movie herself and see if she could go find him or maybe even call him. What was the point of being here if he wasn't even going to show?

*Don't be such a loser,* she told herself. *God, what would Oprah think?*

Maria straightened up and took a deep breath, determined not to pout. She could have a good time without Conner. She was just going to have to find some other way to bump into him before the weekend was over.

"Okay. I can either have one of these Pop-Tarts or a pickle." Megan Sandborn slammed the refrigerator door and leaned back against it. "There is nothing to eat in this house."

11

"I know," Elizabeth Wakefield muttered distractedly.

She wasn't thinking about food. She couldn't. Conner had kissed her. He'd kissed her and then bailed, and now he was upstairs in his room and she was in the kitchen, her stomach doing somersaults. "God, I wish I was home," Elizabeth said under her breath.

Megan's brow creased. "I'm sorry. I'm sure we can find something to eat somewhere," she said, leaning on the table.

"Oh, no. That's not what I meant," Elizabeth said, touching her friend's arm. Megan was the most eager-to-please host in the world, and Elizabeth didn't want her to think she was ungrateful. "I guess I'm just . . . missing my family," she hedged.

Megan's stomach growled audibly, and Elizabeth laughed.

"And I'm just missing food," Megan said.

"Hey, you know what we should do?" Elizabeth said, brightening slightly. "We should get a pizza from Guido's."

"Guido's?" Megan asked.

"Yeah. It's this place in Sweet Valley. When Jess and I were little and Steven was still at home, we used to have family night every Friday night. My parents would order a Guido's pizza, and then we'd all sit around and play board games or something until bedtime. It was kind of dorky, but it was fun."

*And it might just be distracting enough to calm my nerves for five seconds,* Elizabeth thought.

Megan's green eyes took on a faraway look. "I know what you mean. Mom and Conner and I used to do stuff like that, but I can't even remember the last time we all ate dinner together. It feels like it's been forever."

"Tell me about it," Elizabeth said. She got up and pulled out the big yellow phone book from the shelf by the telephone. "I'm going to see if they deliver out here."

"I've got ten bucks up in my room, and I'm pretty sure I can scrounge up some more if we need it," Megan said.

"I've got a few dollars lying around too," Elizabeth said, flipping to the *P* section in the directory. "I don't suppose you have any board games?"

"We've got Monopoly somewhere," Megan said gleefully. "I'm sure I can find it."

"Monopoly?" The voice was loud, sarcastic, and male.

Elizabeth's heart dropped to the floor as she and Megan both turned to find Conner leaning against the door frame.

"You two are going to sit here and play Monopoly on a Saturday night?" Conner asked, clearly mocking the idea. Megan exhaled sharply, causing her strawberry blond bangs to flutter on her forehead. It reminded Elizabeth to breathe.

"Excuse me, but you don't exactly look like you're ready for a glamorous night on the town either, big brother," Megan remarked.

Conner was wearing baggy khaki pants and a white T-shirt. He'd thrown on a blue chambray shirt with fraying cuffs and holes along the hem and left it unbuttoned over the tee. The patented Conner McDermott, intentionally disheveled yet totally sexy look. It seriously irritated Elizabeth.

He checked his watch and shrugged.

"It's only seven-thirty—the night is still young. I was thinking of meeting Tia and Andy for a movie."

*Impressive,* Elizabeth thought. That was the most information she had ever heard Conner give anyone about his personal life, and it was offered freely. Then again, he was talking to his sister—not to her.

Elizabeth shakily turned her attention back to the phone book. Conner obviously wasn't going to acknowledge her presence, and she felt like an idiot standing there gaping at him.

"Hey, I've got an idea," Megan began, sounding excited. "Why don't you stay here and play Monopoly with us, Conner?" Elizabeth froze, but refused to check his reaction.

"What do you think, Liz? Think you can handle it?" Conner asked.

Handle what? Hanging out with him? Playing Monopoly with him? Or not grabbing him, throwing him on the kitchen table, and kissing him like there was no tomorrow?

Elizabeth slowly turned around. There was a flicker of uncertainty in Conner's eyes, and then the mask of amused conceit was there again. The flicker gave her the tad of confidence she needed.

"The question is, can *you* handle it?" she said, raising an eyebrow. Conner blinked, and his gaze wavered slightly. Elizabeth smiled. "I mean, if you're really up to suffering a humiliating defeat in front of your sister . . ."

Conner grinned. "Ooh," he sneered, narrowing his eyes. "I don't think I have a choice now."

Elizabeth blushed and looked at the floor. She couldn't help it. The boy couldn't possibly be any hotter.

Megan did a small jump and clapped.

"Cool!" she said. "This is gonna be great! You guys order the pizza, and I'll go find the Monopoly board." Megan bounded out of the kitchen and into the living room, where Elizabeth saw her start to dig through the cabinets around the TV.

Conner didn't move an inch.

15

"It's really cool that you're giving up a Saturday night for her," he said.

"I don't mind," Elizabeth responded. "I like hanging out with Megan. Besides, I could say the same for you. I'm sure Monopoly isn't exactly your idea of a thrilling activity."

Conner shrugged, keeping his hands in his pockets. "I didn't really have any other plans."

"But I thought you were supposed to meet Tia and Andy for a movie," Elizabeth said nonchalantly. She couldn't help wondering if he'd stayed home for Megan or for her. "Aren't they going to rip you apart for spending a Saturday night with your sister?"

"I can always tell them I was spending it with you," Conner said, lowering his voice into a smooth whisper that sent chills down Elizabeth's spine. Her eyes were locked on his, and she refused to look away.

Conner smirked. "Besides, how could I give up the chance to annihilate you?" he said. With that, he turned and shuffled out of the room, leaving Elizabeth behind.

"Ah, sarcasm," she whispered. "What a jerk."

But Elizabeth couldn't help grinning as she reached for the phone. Conner could play it cool if he wanted, but Elizabeth knew that he was staying in at least partly because of her.

Even if he did just want to kick her butt at Monopoly.

# melissa fox

I still can't believe Tia is the captain of the cheerleading squad. It should have been me, and it would have been if it wasn't for Jessica Wakefield. I know she and Tia went to Coach Laufeld and told her it was my fault Jessica missed the pep rally.

They <u>told</u> on me.

Whiners.

# CHAPTER
## *What Not to Say*

## 2

Jeremy fidgeted with the buttons on his car radio. On the thirteenth lousy station he finally decided just to turn it off. His thoughts were too loud on their own anyway.

All he could think about was Jessica and the fact that she might be deliberately avoiding him. It just didn't make sense. They'd had such a good time the two days they worked together, and he'd really thought that she'd enjoyed his company as much as he had hers. So why would she blow him off?

As he turned down Newbury Lane, Jeremy resolved to talk to Jessica in person. Conclusion jumping never got anyone anywhere.

Jeremy shifted his old Mercedes into third as he approached his house, but before he could make the turn into the driveway, something caught his eye and he slammed on the brakes. There, in the middle of his front lawn, was a huge sign. Jeremy didn't want to believe his eyes, but the large, red letters were unmistakable: For Sale.

Jeremy swallowed back a lump that instantly formed in his throat. *There must be some kind of mistake.*

He stomped on the accelerator, squealing the tires as he sped down the long driveway. He had barely come to a stop before he was out of the car and running up the steps that led into his family's mansion.

His parents' voices resounded through the corridors. They were arguing again. Jeremy made his way through the foyer and into the west-wing living quarters that his family had occupied for the last year. The rest of the house had been closed off entirely in an attempt to lower the utility bills and save money.

"This had to be done, Howard!"

"If you'd just give me a little more time—"

"We're out of time! Can't you see—"

As soon as Jeremy entered the small servants' kitchen, the yelling stopped. Both of his parents turned abruptly to face him, and Jeremy could tell by his mother's expression that she was very, *very* angry. But when his eyes met hers, she turned away, busying herself with the task of tidying up the already immaculate kitchen.

"What's going on?" Jeremy asked, turning his attention to his father, who met his gaze head-on. The morose expression on his dad's face changed quickly to a weak smile.

"Hey, Jeremy, how was the game?" he asked jocularly, as if the scream fest had never happened.

"We lost," Jeremy said shortly, looking his father in the eye. "I guess your interview didn't go very well either." Jeremy hated the bitter tone in his voice and glanced at the floor for a moment, hoping his dad wouldn't catch it.

"It went all right," Mr. Aames said, sounding strained. "I don't think anything will come of it, though. It's just not the kind of work I'm looking for."

Jeremy gritted his teeth, wishing he could lace into his father. He'd daydreamed about it so many times, he could recite the words without thinking.

*What the hell's wrong with you, Dad? Are you just going to sit back and let everything fall apart?*

But as he stared at his father's face, his hands in tight fists at his sides, he knew he couldn't say anything.

Over the past months Mr. Aames had grown increasingly frail. Pale and drawn, he looked so sickly. Lately Jeremy hadn't been able to bring himself to utter even a single harsh word in his father's presence, no matter how much he wanted to just take him by the shoulders and shake him.

Jeremy knew that his father's "disinterest" in the job actually meant that his dad knew he wasn't going to be hired. It was the same every time. Mr. Aames's lack of energy had been difficult for even his wife and son to deal with, let alone a prospective

20

employer. Ever since his father had been fired from his job last year, he'd been either unwilling or unable to get himself back on his feet. Meanwhile the family's savings were fading fast. Jeremy knew his father needed to pull himself together and soon, but he didn't know how to make it happen. And he didn't dare talk to his father about it.

"That's a shame, Dad," he offered finally, trying not to sound disappointed. He patted his father lightly on the shoulder, like he would one of his teammates who had messed up a play. "Next time, huh?"

His father just smiled wanly and shrugged as he started to walk out of the room. "I think I'm going to go lie down for a while," he said, rubbing his forehead. "I've got a headache that just won't let up on me."

Jeremy waited until his father left the room, then turned to face his mom, the pity in his heart turning back into anger. Mrs. Aames had taken a seat at the kitchen table and was sipping her tea slowly, grasping the flowered mug with both hands, as though it were her sole source of comfort.

"So what's going on, Mom?" Jeremy demanded, pulling out a chair and sitting down next to her. "I saw the sign on the lawn. Are you really selling the house?" He tried to keep his voice steady, but he knew his anger was coming through anyway. Mrs. Aames took a long sip from her cup and closed her eyes. "Not now, Jeremy. The girls are over at Katherine's house, and they'll be back soon. I'm too tired to have this conversation and deal with your sisters."

"I'll take care of the girls," Jeremy said tightly. He was relieved that his little sisters, Emma and Trisha, hadn't been around his parents' fight. They'd heard enough yelling lately, and Jeremy was about to provide some more. "Why didn't you tell me you were putting the house on the market?"

Jeremy's mother placed her tea gently down on the table and gazed up at her son. Jeremy noticed how tired her eyes looked, but this wasn't a time for sympathy. He was furious, and he wanted answers.

"I'm sorry, Jeremy," his mother started, shaking her head. "I was going to tell you—"

"When?" Jeremy interrupted, throwing his hands up in the air. "The day after you sold it?"

"No. I wanted to tell you sooner, but I didn't want to worry you unnecessarily," she said, her voice slow and measured. "I decided not to say anything until I was certain we'd have to go through with it."

"Oh, and you just figured that out this afternoon, huh?" Jeremy shouted. "I suppose you had absolutely no idea you were going to put the house on the market until the agent came and nailed the sign to the post on the lawn."

His mother exhaled slowly and closed her eyes. When she opened them, she gave Jeremy a pleading look, but he refused to accommodate her. Instead he sat silently, staring at the floor. He told himself to stop being so immature, but somehow he couldn't help it.

"Your father's not pleased either, as you probably guessed from the argument we were having when you came in, but we have to sell," Mrs. Aames said matter-of-factly. "We've been cutting expenses everywhere we can. We just can't afford this big place anymore." She leaned closer to Jeremy, searching his face. "We're lucky we've managed to stay as long as we have on my salary alone."

Jeremy's jaw began to ache from clenching it. He could feel tears of anger and frustration forming in the corners of his eyes, but he held them back. Rigidly he shook his head, not quite ready to believe what was happening. How could she do this to him—to them? He and his sisters had grown up in this house.

"You should have told me how bad things were before it went this far. I could have done something," he said.

"Jeremy." His mother's voice was soft. "You're only seventeen. You shouldn't have to carry that kind of weight. You should be enjoying yourself, playing football, dating, being a kid. . . ." She reached out and touched Jeremy's hand, attempting to take it in her own, but Jeremy jerked it away.

"Do you know how sick I am of hearing that?" he barked. "I'm not some ten-year-old you have to protect. This affects me just as much as it affects you, and I deserve to know what's going on in my own house."

Jeremy stood up so quickly, he knocked over his chair. He picked it up with one arm and dropped it back into place, then stormed from the kitchen.

All the way up the stairs and down the narrow hallway to his bedroom, he chastised himself for having been so blind to the severity of his family's financial situation. And of course it didn't help that he had just gone off on his mom—as if she needed any more stress in her life.

When he reached his room, Jeremy slammed the door behind him out of sheer frustration. One thought echoed clearly in his mind.

*I should have seen this coming. Maybe then I would have had time to fix it.*

"Are you sure you don't want any more, Maria?" Andy asked sarcastically, gesturing to the nearly full tub of popcorn he was about to dump into the trash can. "Just nine more handfuls and we'll actually have made a small dent in it."

"Yeah, yeah," Maria returned, rolling her eyes. "You were right and I was wrong. I swear I'll never get an extra large again unless Tia promises to eat more."

"Hey, don't lay this one on me," Tia shot back, giving Maria a modest push as they walked down the red-carpeted corridor from the theater to the lobby. Maria lost her balance and fell into Andy, who in turn brushed up against the wall and gave an exaggerated grimace.

"And don't take it out on me just because I'm smarter than you are," he protested, rubbing his shoulder and pretending to be hurt.

"Fine," Maria said, shrugging. "I'll blame it on Conner. Maybe if he had shown up, we wouldn't have been left with so much extra popcorn."

Andy grinned at Tia, and she shook her head ever so slightly.

Maria bit her lip. That was about the fifteenth reference she had made to Conner in the space of two hours.

"What's so funny?" Maria demanded defensively, stopping in the middle of the hall.

"Uh . . . nothing," Andy said, scratching at the back of his neck apprehensively. Maria turned her attention to Tia.

"C'mon, you guys. Why are you picking on me

behind my back?" she asked, placing her hands on her hips. Maria didn't enjoy being the subject of secret glances, unless of course she was being admired by some cute guy at a dance or something. But even then, nine times out of ten she preferred a direct approach.

Of course, when it came to Conner—well, that was different. Sure, she had been going out of her way to run into him and to look cool whenever he was around, but that wasn't really game playing; it was just . . . necessary.

"Let's get out of this crowd," Tia said. She took Maria by the arm and pulled her into a deserted corner next to the concession stand.

"Okay, spill," Maria said. "What's with all the she's-a-psycho looks?"

"All right, I'm just gonna say this," Tia began. "You've been talking about Conner a lot tonight, and it's kind of obvious that you're not over him yet."

Maria looked upward, trying to put forth an aura of indignation, even though what she really felt was more like embarrassment.

"That's ridiculous. Of course I'm over him," Maria countered. Normally she was a great actress, but she was clearly failing in this role. Andy snorted, and Tia raised her eyebrows skeptically.

"Please, Maria," Tia said. "You couldn't even concentrate on the movie. You kept turning around every time the door opened to see if it was him. I thought the girls behind us were going to kill you."

Maria wanted to melt into the floor.

"You noticed that, huh?" she asked, her large, dark brown eyes crinkling in embarrassment.

"It was kind of obvious," Andy said in an apologetic tone.

"Well, it's no big deal," Maria said, crossing her arms over her chest. "I'm fine. I mean, yeah, I still like him a little, but it's hard not to. It's only been like, a week since we broke up." She paused for a minute, feeling sad all over again yet determined to retain her composure.

"But I'm okay with it. Really," she finished.

"Good. Because Conner is the master of unrequited love," Tia said, pulling her thick, dark hair off her shoulders. "I don't think he knows how to . . . requite." Tia looked at Andy. "Is that a word?"

Andy shrugged.

"Anyway, Conner is a good friend, but when it comes to girls, he's never been big on going back," Tia said. "If you know what I mean."

"Well, that was direct," Maria muttered.

"Sorry," Tia said. "I just think you should know the deal."

Andy nodded in agreement, and Maria made herself do the same. Still, she couldn't help thinking that all Conner needed was someone he could really connect with—and they had connected, right?

"You'll be much better off if you just forget about him," Tia added, staring Maria straight in the eye.

"Yeah, you're probably right," Maria said, but she didn't really believe it. She turned her attention to the peeling wallpaper, picking at a fraying edge. She just wanted to change the subject. Talking about Conner so much was making her miss him even more.

"You okay?" Tia asked, resting a hand on Maria's shoulder.

"Yeah. Sure," Maria said, shoving her hands in her pockets. "So what do you guys want to do now?" she asked, moving toward the exit.

"I don't know," Andy said finally, holding the door open for Maria. "I'm kind of beat. And I've still got to clean up after the pool party this afternoon."

"And I'm kind of worn out from the game," Tia added. "I think I'll go home and let this whole captain thing sink in."

Andy led the way to his vintage Cadillac and unlocked the doors.

"Hey—if you want to have coffee in the morning, I'd be all over that. We could go to House of Java," Tia suggested, holding the front seat forward so Maria could crawl in the back.

"Yeah. Liz might be working," Andy said.

*And Conner has been known to go for a cup of coffee in the morning,* Maria thought. *Not that I care.*

"That sounds great," she said. "What time?"

Andy started the car and glanced at Maria in the rearview mirror. "Early," he said. "Tia's impossible if she doesn't get her coffee at dawn."

"Watch it, Marsden," Tia said, swatting Andy's arm. "How about nine-ish?"

"Sounds good to me," Maria said.

"And maybe . . . *maybe* I'll give Conner a call in the morning, but I'm not making any promises," Tia said.

Maria grinned as Tia twisted around in her seat to face her. "But this is the last time I'm doing anything to get the two of you in the same room. After this, you're on your own."

"Thanks, Tia," Maria said sincerely. "I'll never ask again." *And if things go well enough,* she thought, *I'll never need to.*

"I still say that if we had played a little longer, I would have made a comeback," Elizabeth insisted, slumping back into the recliner in the Sandborns' living room.

Conner, who was stretched out on the couch in front of the television, exhaled sharply.

"Give it a rest, Liz," he said. "Just admit that I

am the Monopoly master and you are merely one of my minions."

"As if," Elizabeth shot back with narrowed eyes.

"Ooh, excellent comeback," Conner said, applauding halfheartedly. "Next time why don't you go for something even more sophisticated, like, 'I know you are, but what am I?'"

Elizabeth ignored his remark, mainly because she couldn't think of anything clever to say. Instead she turned to Megan for support, but Megan only looked at her helplessly.

"Sorry, Liz. He may be a jerk," she said, gesturing to her brother, whose face was in full smirk mode, "but you were down to your last dollar."

"Exactly," Elizabeth said, leaning forward in the chair. "I still had a dollar left, which means the game wasn't really over, which means that I could have come back and won, which means Conner didn't officially win anything. All he did is quit while he was ahead so he could pretend that he won." Elizabeth paused for a second to let her theory sink in, and then added, "Besides, I think Conner cheated."

"You never give up, do you?" Conner shook his head, staring at her.

"Not easily," Elizabeth responded as Conner smugly folded his arms behind his head. She tried not to smile. Even when Conner was mocking her, he was captivating.

"I'm pretty beat. I think I'm gonna head upstairs," Megan said, standing up to stretch. She glanced around the room at the empty pizza box, the soda glasses, and the Monopoly money scattered around the floor. "Let's just leave this for tomorrow, okay?"

"Yeah," Conner said, still staring at Elizabeth.

"Good," Megan said, yawning. "I'll see you guys in the morning."

Elizabeth felt like Conner had her under a microscope. She turned to watch Megan walk out so she wouldn't have to keep trying to read his intense expression.

When Megan's bedroom door clicked shut, Elizabeth was acutely aware that she and Conner were very much alone.

Elizabeth sat stiffly in the chair, trying to think of something to say. She tentatively glanced at Conner. He was lying on the sofa with his eyes closed. Elizabeth couldn't believe he'd make himself so vulnerable. Usually when they were together, he was watching her every move, ready to pounce on any misstep or stupid remark. Ready to push her away.

Elizabeth stood up slowly and walked toward the couch as silently as possible. But before she had reached the coffee table, Conner's voice broke the silence.

"What are you doing?" he asked without opening

his eyes. His voice was still sexy, even as he injected a singsong quality into the question. Elizabeth stopped abruptly, her body rigid.

"I was just getting the remote," she said. "I thought I'd see if there were any old movies on or anything. Do you mind?"

"Nope. Be my guest," Conner returned, rolling over on his side to face the TV, his eyes still closed. "You should sit over here, though. View's better."

He sounded so casual, so calm, but Elizabeth nearly crumbled at his words. Somehow she managed to cover her surprise with a cough. Was Conner coming on to her? She couldn't be sure—he might not even be fully awake.

"All right," she said, lifting the remote gingerly from the table and walking toward the couch. Since Conner was stretched out over the full length of the sofa and hadn't made any effort to make room for her, she opted to sit on the floor in front of him. She chose a spot near his chest where she wouldn't be blocking his view of the TV if he ever decided to open his eyes.

His right hand was tucked under his head so that his elbow stuck out, and when Elizabeth leaned back, she could almost feel his arm against her neck.

She clicked on the TV, surfing through the channels without even noticing what was on. She was too focused on the proximity of Conner's arm to concentrate on anything else. Every now and then he shifted his position slightly, causing all of the hairs on her neck to stand up as his elbow grazed her skin. She could hear his breath and almost feel it on her ear. She desperately wanted to turn around and kiss him or at least touch him, but she couldn't find the will to move.

Then Elizabeth felt something on her left shoulder. Conner had brought his arm down so that his hand was resting there. Elizabeth's skin tingled.

*Oh my God. Breathe, breathe, breathe.*

"Are you all right?" Conner asked, his voice sounding more tender than she had ever heard it before—or maybe it was just sleepier.

"I'm fine," Elizabeth blurted out, knowing she had just made the understatement of the year.

*Do it now,* she thought, steeling herself. *You'll never get a better opportunity than this.*

She closed her eyes and took a deep breath, allowing herself to fully absorb the weight and feel of Conner's hand against her shoulder. His thumb had begun to move slowly at the base of her neck, and she felt her whole body throbbing as the blood coursed through her veins. Finally she found her voice.

"Um, can I ask you something?" she managed, hoping she didn't sound as nervous as she actually was. Conner didn't even flinch. His hand remained steady on her shoulder, and his thumb began to move with more certainty now, massaging her shoulder.

"Shoot," he said, his voice barely above a whisper.

"What—," she started, but before her mouth could finish, her mind wimped out.

"—time do you think your mom will be home?" she finished, flinching. She was as surprised as Conner evidently was by what had come out.

His thumb stopped abruptly, and he withdrew his hand from Elizabeth's shoulder. Slowly he sat up on the sofa and placed his feet on the floor. Then he leaned forward, his elbows resting on his knees, and faced her.

"I don't know—why?" he asked, appearing a bit annoyed. His voice had changed; it was no longer tender, or sleepy, or whatever it had been before. Elizabeth shook her head. She had no reason for asking apart from her own stupidity.

"I—I was just wondering," she stammered. "I'd hate for her to come home and find the house such a mess," she added lamely.

"She wouldn't even notice," Conner said bitterly. Elizabeth turned to look at him, puzzled.

"It's too dark in here," he added in explanation.

"Oh," Elizabeth said.

"I'm gonna call it a night," Conner said, standing and shoving his hands in his pockets. He looked at her briefly, then shook his head and left the room.

Elizabeth tried desperately to think of something she could say to make him come back, but she knew the moment was over.

The water turned on in the upstairs bathroom, and Elizabeth boosted herself up onto the couch. She let her head fall into her hands.

"What time will your mother be home?" she repeated in a quiet, mocking tone. "It's like I'm subconsciously trying to sabotage my chances with him."

And from the way Conner had bolted out of the room, her subconscious had succeeded.

# Conner McDermott

All right. This is getting out of hand. Maybe I was half asleep, but thats no excuse. And if Liz wasn't so damned neurotic, who knows what would have happened?

I've never had a problem with self-control.

This ends now.

# CHAPTER

*Not Quite Life-Altering*
**3**
*Decisions*

Jeremy stopped the lawn mower under a large oak tree at the edge of his family's property. Lifting the bottom of his gray jersey, he wiped the sweat from his face and then glanced at his watch. Eight twenty-two A.M. It had taken him only forty-five minutes to do half of the front lawn—a task that normally took at least an hour and a half. But he was flying today, and he knew why. It was all about angry adrenaline.

After his argument with his mother, there was no chance of sleep. At 6 A.M. Jeremy had given up altogether, opting to go for a run and then start on the lawn.

Ever since the family had dismissed the gardeners along with the rest of the staff, Sunday mornings had been reserved for yard work. And today mowing the lawn had afforded him the extra benefit of being able to tip over the For Sale sign before anyone had a chance to see it.

"Hey, Jeremy, my lad," a voice called from the walkway that passed by the front of the Aameses' estate. Jeremy looked up to see Mr. O'Doole, one of his parents' longtime friends and neighbors. He lived one block up in an equally impressive mansion—a house Jeremy was fairly certain wouldn't be going on the market anytime soon.

"Hello, Mr. O'Doole," Jeremy called back, waving. "How are you today, sir?"

"Can't complain, can't complain," the older man responded, stroking his white beard. "You, on the other hand," he said, wagging a long, bony index finger at Jeremy, "you shouldn't be out here doing this lawn all by yourself. It's too big for one boy! Don't you have landscapers for this sort of work?"

Part of Jeremy wanted to tell Mr. O'Doole the truth—that his family couldn't afford to live here anymore, let alone hire someone to care for the estate. At least then he wouldn't have to keep pretending there was nothing wrong. But a larger part of him was still hoping that he could fix everything before anyone had to find out how dire the situation had become. The larger part won.

"Hey! I'm a machine," he joked, flexing one arm to make a muscle. "Besides, it keeps me in shape for football."

Mr. O'Doole laughed. He reminded Jeremy of the sort of grandfatherly figure that always appeared in children's storybooks.

"In that case, I've got a couple of acres up the

street that could use a bit of tending," Mr. O'Doole jested. Even from twenty feet away, the twinkle in his gray-blue eyes was visible.

"Just say the word," Jeremy offered, even though he knew his neighbor hadn't been serious. "I can always use the exercise."

"If you like it that much, you should start up a landscaping business," Mr. O'Doole said with a wink. "Might as well earn a buck with all that energy of yours."

Jeremy half smiled. "I'll take that into consideration."

"Enjoy the day, Jeremy," Mr. O'Doole said as he started off. "Don't work too hard."

"Talk to you later," Jeremy called after him. *If I still live here next time you come by, that is,* he thought. Jeremy looked around at the acres of grass that still needed mowing.

It could wait. Mr. O'Doole was right. There were more useful things he could do with his time. More profitable things.

Jeremy pushed the lawn mower back to the garden house and headed inside to take a quick shower. When he was dry and dressed, he rushed to the kitchen. His parents hadn't gotten up yet, and he didn't want to be around when they did. He'd have to explain where he was going, and he knew they would object. This was a time for solutions, not more problems.

Jeremy grabbed his car keys from the small shelf by the front door. The earlier he got to House of Java, the better his odds were. Ally was always in a good mood after her first cup of coffee.

Maria threw her head back dramatically, aware that Tia, Angel, and Andy were wondering why she was laughing so hard at Andy's somewhat lame joke.

But her big smile was her best feature. And they'd understand soon enough.

Maria looked over Tia's shoulder. Conner had come in just moments ago, and now he was at the counter, ordering his coffee.

"What are you staring at?" Tia asked Maria, turning around to see for herself. Conner had just grabbed his coffee and started toward their table. When Tia spotted him, she waved and then turned back to Maria and shook her head.

"Girl, you are hopeless," she said, adjusting the strap of her red tank top.

"Cut her a break, baby," Angel said. "She's in love." Andy chuckled, but Maria was getting edgy. Conner was only five feet away.

"Shhh!" she hissed, kicking Tia under the table. Tia scowled, but she didn't give Maria away. Hopefully Conner had missed their little exchange.

"Andy. Tee," he said when he was close enough, nodding to each of them in greeting. He clasped

Angel's outstretched hand as he made his way around the table. "Hey, man, how's it goin'?"

"Not bad," Angel returned. "You?"

"Can't complain," Conner said. Then he turned to Maria.

"Hey," he said, barely making eye contact. Maria noticed that his tone seemed a little distant, but then again, it was early, and Conner didn't exactly strike her as a chipper morning person.

Maria watched Conner take in the seating arrangement and notice that the only empty chair at the table was conveniently located next to Maria. He paused for only a moment before he grabbed the chair by its top rung and flipped it around. He straddled the seat as he sat down.

There was a hole in the left knee of his jeans that opened wider as his leg bent, exposing a section of flesh. He was wearing a black T-shirt that clung just enough to suggest the definition of his chest and stomach without actually appearing tight. But Maria already knew that he was in good shape. What amazed her was his effortless grace. He never appeared awkward or uncomfortable, and every move he made seemed deliberate.

"So what happened to you last night, man?" Andy asked.

Conner took a sip of his coffee. "I just kicked back at home with . . . Megan."

"Aw. Isn't that cute?" Tia said. "Brotherly bonding."

Conner glanced at Tia. "Something like that."

*God, he's amazing,* Maria thought. *Hanging out with his sister on a Saturday night* and *admitting it to his friends?*

Tia nudged Maria's ankle with her toe, and Maria was instantly aware that she was gaping. *Say something,* she told herself.

"Was Liz around when you left this morning?" she asked. Conner visibly tensed, and Maria wanted to smack herself. Conner and Elizabeth did not get along. Why did she have to mention Elizabeth?

"I don't know. I'm not her keeper," Conner said.

Maria tried not to flinch at his harsh tone. She looked at Tia for help, but everyone else was in uncomfortable-silence mode.

"Hey, I'm having a few people over after school tomorrow," Andy said finally. "Are you guys up for it?"

Conner took another sip from his coffee and nodded. Maria looked at his slightly tousled hair. The just-rolled-out-of-bed-and-came-straight-here look. God, he was sexy.

"Yeah, sounds doable," Conner responded. "I don't think I have anything else going on."

"Cool," Maria responded impulsively. "I mean, it should be cool. Hanging tomorrow. At Andy's." *Foot in mouth.*

Conner glanced at her out of the corner of his

eye. "I think I'm gonna take this to go," he said, standing.

Maria felt her face go red. She hadn't even had a chance to *really* embarrass herself yet.

"Conner—," Tia began.

Conner shot her a silencing look.

He turned his chair around and pushed it in, moving away from Maria.

"Later," Conner said as he walked toward the door.

"See ya, Conner," Andy and Tia responded, almost in unison. Angel just stared at Maria in pity.

Humiliation. Maria was beginning to become familiar with it. She buried her head in her hands and shook it back and forth, her curls bouncing around her face.

"Oh my God. I'm such an idiot," she whimpered. Her voice was muffled behind her palms.

"It wasn't that bad," Andy finally offered.

"No. I made him uncomfortable. I babbled."

"No, really. He's right, Maria," Angel agreed, his tone sympathetic. "It's really kind of sweet that you get so nervous around him. Conner doesn't know what he's missing. It's his loss."

Maria tried to smile. "But I sounded so desperate. Conner must think I'm a total loser."

"Oh, come on, Maria," Tia jumped in. "You're better off without him anyway."

"I'd be saner, that's for sure," Maria said, sitting

back heavily in her chair and taking a long sip of coffee.

"I know what will cheer you up," Tia said, leaning forward and raising her eyebrows. "A mall run. I've got to get some new shoes to wear with my black dress. Angel and I are going to dinner tonight." She grinned, leaning closer to her boyfriend.

"Oh, yeah. Tell her some more happy-couple stories. That ought to cheer her right up," Andy said sarcastically. Tia and Angel glared at him.

"Sorry," Andy muttered. "But it's true."

"Thanks, Tia, but I think I'm just gonna head home and dive into my homework," Maria said. "I've been such a social failure lately that it would probably be better if I just avoid contact with the outside world for the rest of the day."

"Are you sure?" Tia asked, pulling a chunk from her blueberry muffin and popping it into her mouth.

"Yeah. Besides, I've got a major project to start in history with Ken 'Night of the Walking Dead' Matthews. I have a feeling I'm going to be doing more than my share of the work, so I need to get some other stuff out of the way," Maria said. Right now she just wanted to go home. She was feeling a bit like the walking dead herself.

"Nice nickname," Angel said. "Who's Ken?"

Maria sighed. "That's a loaded question. He

used to be this superpopular ultrajock, but his girlfriend died in the earthquake, and he hasn't been the same since."

Angel whistled. "God, that's sad."

"Yeah, it is," Maria agreed, "but it's still hard to deal with him. I mean, he won't talk to anyone or do anything—it's like he's not even trying to make things better. And I know people always say these things take time, but that doesn't help me with my history project."

"Good point," Angel responded.

"So no mall?" Tia interjected.

"No mall. No crowds. Not much opportunity to embarrass myself doing homework." Maria laughed halfheartedly, shaking her head. She was amazed by her own absurd behavior around Conner. This was the last time she was going to fall in love at first sight. It really was almost humorous—at least it would be if it were happening to someone else.

It was time to surround herself with work. No Conners allowed. If she could distract herself with academics for a while, maybe she could cool down around him and stop acting like such a groupie.

And if she could accomplish that, maybe she'd actually have a shot at getting him back.

Jeremy pulled open the glass door and strode purposefully toward the counter at House of Java.

According to the clock behind the counter, it was nine-fifteen.

*Perfect,* Jeremy thought. About now, Ally would be settling into her desk, second cup of coffee in hand, ready to start putting together the work schedule for the following week. It was the ideal time to talk to her.

"Ally in back?" he asked Corey. To his surprise she didn't have any sarcastic comments for him. She just nodded and continued working. Jeremy made a mental note to ask her later if anything was wrong. Silence was not something he'd come to expect from Corey.

"Thanks," he called as he walked around the counter toward the back of the building. Ally was right where she was supposed to be.

Her straight brown hair was pulled back from her face and held in an untidy bun by two pencils at cross angles. She was wearing her typical Sunday outfit—old tennis shoes, a pair of tattered jeans, and a gray, zippered sweatshirt, all of which looked comfortable enough to sleep in.

Ally was in her late twenties, but Jeremy thought she could easily have passed for a teenager.

"Hey, Jer," she greeted him. "What are you doing here? I can't pay you if you're not on the schedule."

Jeremy amended his previous thought. She

could pass as a teenager as long as she didn't speak. Maybe it was Ally's personality, or maybe it was just the stress of managing her mom's café, but she completely lacked the customary carefree attitude. Every time Jeremy talked to her, he couldn't help feeling like there was a time limit on the conversation.

"I came in to talk to you," Jeremy said. He thought she'd appreciate him getting right to the point. "I want you to give me more hours." He saw the skeptical look on Ally's face and knew what was coming before he heard it.

"Jeremy, we've had this discussion before, and I've already upped your hours once. I can't give you any more time without cutting back someone else's hours, and that's not fair to them." She paused, looking at him with wonder. "Besides, don't you have school, football, girlfriends . . . you know, a life to lead? You can't spend all of your time working."

Jeremy tensed up. Why did everyone seem to have the same argument? Of course he had a life to lead, but that life included a house his family couldn't afford and a mother who looked so tired sometimes that it made him want to cry. Football and girlfriends were hardly at the top of the list.

But Jeremy wasn't about to share any of that with Ally—or anyone else for that matter. Even though at times he wondered how much longer he could go on pretending everything was fine.

"Look, I could really use the hours," Jeremy said, his voice void of emotion. "Just see what you can do."

Ally looked back at him. "Are you okay, Jeremy? Do you want to talk about something?"

Jeremy appreciated the effort, but if he was going to spill his guts to anyone, it wasn't going to be his manager. "The only thing I want to talk about is my new schedule."

Ally sighed. "I'll try, but I can't promise you anything."

"Thanks, Ally. Call me if you come up with something."

Jeremy turned and walked out the door, his pace slow and heavy. "Not exactly a screaming success," he muttered as he headed for his car. His head was hanging as he walked around a corner, and he slammed right into another pedestrian.

"Sorry," Jeremy said, catching the girl's arm and steadying her. She bent down to pick up the books he had knocked out of her arms, and when she stood to look at him, her expression mirrored his surprise.

"Jeremy!" she said, smiling.

"Jessica?" he responded, even more surprised by how happy she seemed to see him.

"I'm sorry," she apologized. She looked down and started fidgeting with her books. "I—I didn't mean to run into you. Are you working this morning?"

"No, I just came in to talk to Ally about the schedule," Jeremy said, his voice tentative. Jessica was acting way nervous. "Are you okay?"

"Sure. Why?" she asked, avoiding his gaze.

"It's just—well, you ran off so suddenly yesterday. I thought something might be wrong."

"Oh, that," she said finally, looking back at him. Her blue-green eyes were overflowing with uncertainty.

"Yeah," Jeremy said, dying for a clue as to what he should and shouldn't say. He didn't want to scare her away again, but he didn't want to betray his feelings in case she hated him. Why did she look so scared? "I was worried about you," he said finally.

"You were?" Jessica asked. Then she laughed, and Jeremy's nerves calmed slightly. "I'm sorry, I just . . . I wasn't feeling well, so I went home." She smiled slightly. "Hard to cheer when you're physically ill."

Jeremy's brow wrinkled. She didn't look like she'd been sick.

"I have good news today, though," Jessica said, beaming. Jeremy had to smile. She was too beautiful not to smile at.

"What's that?" he asked.

"I'm going to be working here in Elizabeth's place—permanently," Jessica said.

"Really?" Jeremy asked. *Eager much?* he chided himself.

"See, Liz was supposed to work for me yesterday at my old job, but she skipped my shift and got me fired," Jessica explained. "So when I called her this morning to tell her about it, she called the manager here. Ally, right?"

Jeremy nodded.

"Yeah, she called Ally. Apparently they didn't need another employee, so to make a long story short, Ally agreed to let me work here instead of Liz. As me this time, of course." Jessica took a deep breath. "I'm babbling, aren't I?"

"Just a little," Jeremy said.

Jessica laughed. "So, aren't you psyched to have a coffee guru like me by your side?"

"It's amazing." Jeremy shook his head.

"It's pretty funny, isn't it?"

"It is, but that isn't what I was talking about," he said.

"Ooookay. What were you talking about?" Jessica asked.

"It's just—it's amazing what you do for my mood," Jeremy said. Jessica blushed and looked down. Jeremy hoped he hadn't gone too far.

"The feeling's mutual," she said, fixated on the ground until the words were out. Then she stared at him shyly for a moment before looking away again.

"I guess I better get to work," Jessica said finally. "I don't want to be late on my first day."

"Absolutely not," Jeremy agreed. "You have to keep this job long enough to work another shift with me."

Jessica grinned at him as she walked by.

"You better watch what you say," she warned him, opening the café door. "I have a feeling there's another carton of milk in the walk-in with your name on it."

Jeremy laughed as she disappeared inside. "Now I *really* need to get more hours."

# Maria Slater

You know how in <u>Romeo and Juliet,</u> Romeo finds Juliet in the tomb and commits suicide because he thinks she's dead? And then five seconds later, Juliet wakes up, finds him dead, and commits suicide herself? Well, I've played Juliet in a couple of community-theater productions, and that part's always bugged me. Not because they both kill themselves or anything, but because they do it too quickly.

I mean, Juliet's body isn't even cold when Romeo touches her, but does the boy pause to take a pulse? No. He just gives up and drinks his poison. And then Juliet wakes up, sees him lying there, and kills herself too. Maybe if she had tried a little mouth-to-mouth or gone for help or <u>something,</u> he would have lived. But no, they both just took a quick look, made an assumption, and gave up. If they'd tried a little harder, maybe they could've had the everlasting love they both wanted so much, but instead they lost it all.

Well, I'm not about to make the same mistake. What if Conner is my one true love? What if we were meant to be together? Relationships don't just happen they take work. And I can tell you one thing: I'm not going to blow it by drinking poison.

# CHAPTER 4

## *Glimmer of Hope*

*Gotta love Monday morning,* Maria thought as she watched throngs of students shuffle by, their eyelids half shut, as though they hadn't quite woken up from the weekend. *I never realized how rare it is to be a morning person.*

Maria had practically sprinted out of homeroom and down the hall to arrive at her AP history class five minutes early in hopes that she and Ken could start planning out their project right away. But as she stood by the door to the classroom, she realized her chances were slim to none.

*What was I thinking? Ken never gets here before the bell,* she admonished herself. If he bothered to show at all.

Maria sighed. She craned her neck to get a better view down the hallway. Conner's history class was just a few doors down, and there was a good chance she could catch a glimpse of him walking in. She wasn't going to throw herself at him anymore, but that didn't mean she had to avoid him *completely.*

Maria stood on her toes. She thought she recognized Conner's short, tousled hair and his casual stride in the distance. She was just about to lean out for a better look when she heard Mr. Ford call to her from inside the room. She tried to sneak a peek anyway, but when she heard Mr. Ford's voice again—more commanding this time—she knew she'd better get inside. No sense ticking off the teacher first thing in the morning.

"I'm sorry, did you call me?" Maria asked, approaching Mr. Ford's desk. The older, bearded man was shuffling through numerous papers and folders on his desk.

"Yes, Ms. Slater, I did," Mr. Ford said evenly, his voice crisp. "I wanted to inquire about your project. Have you and Ken made any progress yet?"

Maria's eyes widened. The project had just been assigned on Friday. What did the man expect? Thankfully, her mouth articulated a better answer.

"We both had prior commitments over the weekend, but we're scheduling our first study date for early this week," Maria said, only partially lying. She did plan to set up a study date right away; she just hadn't consulted Ken about it yet.

"Excellent. I'm glad you're planning to start early, but there's another matter I wanted to address with you as well," Mr. Ford responded, lowering his voice.

"Okay," Maria said, mimicking his confidential tone.

"Certainly you've noticed that Mr. Matthews hasn't been himself lately," Mr. Ford said.

Maria nodded. Who hadn't? The transformation from star quarterback to barely there had hardly been subtle.

"I'm afraid he seems to be withdrawing, and I'm hoping that pairing the two of you together on this project will help to stir him from his dormancy," her teacher continued.

"Oh," Maria responded. Was Mr. Ford actually asking her to play social worker here? Did he expect her to coax Ken into opening up?

"I'm simply hoping that you can draw him out a bit, talk with him, get him to contribute something to the project. After all," he added, "a portion of your grade depends on your collaboration as partners. I don't want to see a one-sided project."

*Great,* Maria thought. *Now my grade depends on my ability to play tutor and therapist.*

"I'll do what I can," she promised, glancing up at the clock. Damn. There was less than a minute before the bell. Conner was probably already in his class. Maria turned to take her seat just as Ken strolled through the door.

"No time like the present," Mr. Ford said.

"Right." Maria was barely able to keep the sarcasm out of her voice.

"Hey, Ken. We need to set up a study date," Maria said, intercepting Ken before he had a chance to withdraw into himself. He gave her a blank stare. "You know, for our project? Our history project?" Maria coaxed.

Finally a dim light seemed to go on somewhere in Ken's head.

"Oh, yeah," he mumbled, his voice barely audible. "This afternoon?" he suggested.

"I'm busy today," Maria answered, not wanting to give up her opportunity to bump into Conner at Andy's informal gathering. "But I could do tomorrow afternoon or Wednesday."

"I don't think I can," Ken answered, running a hand through his blond hair as he shifted his feet impatiently. "Can we just set something up later?"

Maria glanced at Mr. Ford, who was obviously listening to the conversation. She knew he would be less than impressed if she couldn't even get her first study date with Ken set. Her grade had probably dropped ten points in the last ten seconds. Ken turned away and started to move toward his desk.

"Wait, Ken," she said before he could sit down. "Actually, this afternoon is fine. How about right after school in the library?" Maria couldn't believe it. She had just given up an afternoon with Conner to study history with Ken Matthews. Ken, who she was going to have to lead by the hand through this entire assignment.

"Whatever," was all Ken offered in response, but to Maria's surprise, he actually took out an assignment notebook and wrote it down.

Maybe this wouldn't be so bad after all.

Jeremy pulled his football jersey over his head and smoothed the sleeves over his shoulder pads. The whole team was gathered in the Big Mesa boys' locker room for a prepractice review of their Saturday game. Coach Anderson had already started in with his typical day-after-the-loss speech, full of lines like, "We'll get 'em next time," and "Let's learn from our mistakes."

Eleven little $x$'s and eleven little $o$'s had been drawn on the chalkboard so Coach could go over every failed play and demonstrate how Sweet Valley had managed to slip through their defense and block their offense.

As a senior who had three years of varsity ball behind him, Jeremy had heard most of it a hundred times by now. He leaned forward, one leg up on the bench with his elbow rested on top of it, and stared blankly toward the front of the room. *If I work every night after practice until closing and then all day Saturday and Sunday, I could make ...*

Jeremy ran the numbers over and over, each time throwing in a few more hours that he might be able to squeeze in before school, after football season, or during vacations, but it never seemed like enough.

Jeremy closed his eyes in frustration. He had been a complete idiot to think for even one second that he could save his family's mansion with a part-time job pouring coffee. Hell, even a full-time job pouring coffee wasn't going to make much of a difference. Jeremy racked his brain, trying to figure out what he could do to stop life as he knew it from slipping away, but he was clueless.

Suddenly he realized that the locker room had gone silent. Jeremy pulled himself out of his reverie just in time to notice that everyone had turned in his direction. The whole team was staring at him. Time for the captain's speech.

"All right, guys," Jeremy said without missing a beat. "We can't let one defeat shape our attitude for the next nine games. Because if we hit that field next Saturday thinking of ourselves as an oh-and-one team, we're dead before we even start."

A few of the team members started nodding, giving Jeremy all the encouragement he needed to say the words they were expecting to hear. "Instead we need to look at that loss as our motivation to do better. Just like a runner who bombs the first lap in his race has to run twice as fast to win, we have to go out there for the next nine weeks and give twice as much as we think we can. We need to practice twice as hard, think twice as smart, and play twice as tough!"

By now Jeremy could feel the energy in the locker room escalating. His teammates started to cheer in response.

"So let's get out there and tear up that field! No mercy! No fear! And the next time we're in Sweet Valley, we'll be their worst nightmare!" With his last words, Jeremy pointed his index finger and brought his hand down in a hard, sweeping gesture to the cheers and howls of his teammates. In one massive movement the locker room emptied and the players jogged out onto the field, yelling and high fiving one another as they started their warm-up laps.

Jeremy trailed the pack, not half as psyched up as everyone else appeared to be. For him, the speech had been automatic. As captain for the second year in a row, Jeremy had given plenty of inspirational speeches to his team, and at this point the enthusiasm had become something he could turn on with a moment's notice. Or even without notice, as he had proved today.

As they reached the field, Jeremy noticed his best friend, Trent Maynor, hanging back.

"Nice speech," Trent said, clapping Jeremy on the back. "For a second I didn't think you were awake in there."

"What can I say? I was just thinking about my speech," Jeremy kidded.

"Well, it worked," Trent said, taking off at a jog. "Think you can keep up with me, Captain?"

"Eat my dust," Jeremy said sprinting past his friend.

As Trent caught up, Jeremy couldn't help wondering how he'd managed to snow even his best friend. Apparently he had become quite a performer over the last year. Between regularly psyching up his team and pretending everything at home was great, he was getting more rehearsal time than the drama club. All in all, Jeremy was quite an accomplished actor.

Too bad there wasn't any money in it.

Maria stared at the institutional brown-and-white clock on the library wall, watching the seconds tick away. She had been waiting for Ken for over an hour, but—big shock—he had blown her off.

The worst part was that she had just spent sixty minutes doodling in her notebook and staring at the clock when she could have been having a fabulous time at Andy's party, hanging out with Tia, Angel, Andy, and hmmm . . . wasn't someone else going to be there? Oh, yeah, *Conner!*

"That's it. I'm outta here," Maria said quietly. She stood up from the table, swearing under her breath.

If she hurried, she could still be at Andy's by

four. She grabbed her crocheted purse from the back of her chair and headed out.

Of course, Maria was certain that with the way things had been going lately, she'd either miss Conner by five seconds or cause him to bolt five seconds after she got there. Still, it was worth a try. Besides, she was already dressed for the occasion.

Maria had agonized over her outfit that morning just in case she bumped into Conner in the hall. And in her hip-hugging black trousers and a clingy, white knit tank top, she was definitely styling. Add the fact that her chunky heels put her over the supermodel-worthy six-foot-tall mark, and how could he resist? Maria forced herself not to answer that question.

Maria walked toward the student parking lot, a slight spring in her step. But as she neared her green Taurus wagon, she could tell that something wasn't right. A moment later it registered. Her left front tire was completely flat.

Maria's jaw dropped. She felt like pitching all of her books and throwing a temper tantrum right there in the middle of the parking lot. Could this day get any worse?

Just then, she was startled by a voice directly behind her.

"Bummer," was all he said, but Maria knew instantly who it was. Her heart leaped.

"Totally, especially considering that I don't

have a spare," she said, proud of her complete composure. She turned to see that Conner was only about three feet away. "What are you doing here? I thought you'd be at Andy's by now. You and everyone else, that is," she added quickly.

"Got held up," he said, with a slight shrug. No explanation, no small talk, and seemingly no need to fill the silence with chatter.

Maria fought to remain in control of herself, focusing on her car. After all, it was hard to get all doe-eyed and giggly with a flat tire looming in front of her and the knowledge that there was no spare in the trunk. Maria looked up at Conner blankly, trying to figure out if she should call her parents or a garage, only half aware of him glancing back and forth between her and her car.

"Want a lift?" he offered, to Maria's surprise.

"Seriously?" she asked.

Conner smirked. "Seriously," he repeated.

"Sure," she said, instructing herself to stay cool. "Are you headed to Andy's?"

"I was thinking about it. You?"

"Yeah. At least I was until I came out here and found my flat tire. But if you don't mind a passenger, maybe you could drop me off. I'm sure I can find a ride home with someone else from there," she added, congratulating herself for her restraint.

Conner nodded. "Let's go. You can call a tow truck when we get there."

Maria walked slowly over to Conner's car, which was only a few spaces away. A million different ideas popped into her head as she tried to think of some way to strike up an intelligent conversation, but nothing seemed appropriate. Thankfully, when Conner unlocked the doors and let her in, there were a few tapes lying on the seat. She scanned the titles. Nirvana, Pearl Jam, Bob Dylan. And then one in particular caught her eye.

"Patsy Cline?" she said, grinning as Conner started the car and pulled out of the parking lot. He glanced over at the tape she was holding.

"Yeah, so?" he asked. Maria lowered one eyebrow and looked at him skeptically.

"She just doesn't seem to fit in with the rest of your music. Don't tell me you're a closet country fan," she remarked. But Conner didn't seem to be aware of her slightly flirtatious tone.

"Not really," he answered, keeping his focus on the road in front of him. Maria decided to drop the subject.

Unfortunately she was unable to come up with a new one. The ride to Andy's was mostly silent, but Maria wasn't disappointed. At least she had managed fifteen minutes alone with Conner without making a fool of herself. It was a start, and maybe it would make him realize that he could just relax around her and be himself. Then she'd be able to make some real progress.

When Conner finally pulled into Andy's driveway, he kept the engine running. Maria looked over at him, waiting for him to turn it off, but he was just staring forward.

"Aren't you going to get out?" she asked tentatively. Maybe he was sitting still because he wanted to talk to her. Conner tilted his head to the side and reached out the window to adjust his sideview mirror.

"No, I think I'm gonna head home," he answered finally. He paused as if he were thinking something over, then he turned to face Maria. "Can you just tell Andy I'll call him later?"

"Sure," Maria answered as evenly as possible, managing to disguise her disappointment. She popped the trick handle on her door and stepped out. But when she reached back in for her things, she couldn't let him go without asking at least one question. "Was it something I said?"

Conner looked back at her seriously for a moment, his gorgeous, unreadable green eyes trained on hers.

"Yeah, it was that Patsy Cline crack," he said with a straight face. Maria froze, her eyes large and mortified.

But then Conner's blank expression turned into a half smile. "Kidding," he added in a low, gravelly voice.

Maria let out a sigh of relief. She flashed

Conner a bright smile as she gathered her things and stepped back.

"Thanks for the ride," she said, leaning down to look in at him once more.

"No problem," Conner said. Maria slammed the door and turned to walk up the driveway.

She took a deep breath of the fresh salt air and smiled.

Will pulled his Blazer to a stop in front of Desmond's Total Auto and stared at the neon sign. Angel's Toyota was parked out front.

"What am I doing here?" Will muttered to himself, still gripping the steering wheel. But he knew exactly what he was doing. He was going to see an old friend. Someone who was at least slightly removed from Sweet Valley High. Someone who just might be able to give him impartial advice and keep his mouth shut about it. The problem was, he hadn't made an effort to hang out with Angel since Angel graduated last spring. Who knew if the guy would even talk to him?

Will killed the engine and climbed out of his car. There was only one way to find out.

He crossed the parking lot and swung open the door to the tiny, but relatively clean, front office. Angel's father was behind the counter, studying some papers on a clipboard. He looked up and grinned.

"William!" Mr. Desmond said, thrusting out his hand. "It's good to see you."

"You too," Will said, shaking the older man's hand. Mr. Desmond's nails were permanently lined with black stains, but his handshake was firm and grease-free. "Is Angel around?"

"He's inside working on an old Caddy," Mr. Desmond answered. "You having car troubles?"

"Nope," Will said, shoving his hands in the back pockets of his jeans. "Girl troubles."

Mr. Desmond smiled knowingly. "Then Angel's the man to see. I may be married twenty years, but that boy knows more about women than I ever will. Go bother him." Mr. Desmond shooed Will toward the door that connected the office to the garage.

"Thanks," Will said with a laugh. The garage was a cavernous space, lined with workbenches and shelves. Every available surface was stacked with parts, cans of various auto fluids, rags, grease-stained manuals, and dozens of unidentifiable items. Of course, Angel always knew what to do with every item on hand—a skill that never ceased to amaze Will.

He found Angel's legs sticking out from under a burgundy Cadillac. The clicking of a socket wrench echoed through the garage.

"Hey, Jammer," Will said, kicking Angel's ankle. The wrench clicking stopped. "Well, if it isn't the long-lost QB." Angel's voice was muffled. Will took a step back as Angel rolled out from under the car on a dolly. Any nervousness Will might have felt over whether Angel would give him the cold shoulder immediately flew out the window. Angel was grinning from ear to ear.

"How are you, man?" Angel asked, hoisting himself up. He pulled a rag from the pocket of his dingy jumpsuit and wiped his hands.

"Okay," Will said, leaning back against the Cadillac. He kicked at the concrete floor with the toe of his sneaker. "Well, not okay."

"The whole love-triangle thing got you down?" Angel asked, slapping Will's shoulder.

Will reflexively checked his jacket for grease and found none. "Tia's kept you informed, huh?" he asked.

"This is Tia we're talking about," Angel reminded him. "Mouth with an unstoppable motor?"

"Right," Will said with a laugh. "Well, whatever she told you was probably true."

"I hope not, for your sake," Angel said with a smirk.

"All right. The deal is, I went out with Jessica behind Melissa's back. Melissa found out about it and went all psychotic trying to . . . I don't know . . . *destroy* Jessica. And now I want to break up with Melissa, but I feel guilty because I cheated on her."

Angel shook his head and laughed. He plopped down on a stool, facing Will, and looked him directly in the eye.

"My understanding of the deal is this," he said, crossing his arms over his chest. "You liked Jessica, but you didn't have the guts to break up with Melissa, so you cheated on her. Then you didn't have the guts to stand up to Melissa, so you let her trash Jessica. And now you don't have the guts to either help Jessica *or* break up with Melissa." Angel nodded, obviously satisfied by his assessment. "Yep, it's all about you being gutless."

Will felt his cheeks flare and looked at the ground. "Knew I could count on you for a reality check."

"Dude, you should have come to me weeks ago," Angel said.

"What would you have told me then?" Will asked.

"I would've told you to dump the manipulative ball and chain and go for the blonde," Angel said.

Will laughed. "And now?"

Angel shrugged and looked at the ceiling as if he was pondering the answer. "Dump the manipulative ball and chain and go for the blonde." He grinned, his brown eyes shining.

"It's not that easy," Will said, wishing it were. "Melissa and I have been together longer than you and Tia," he pointed out. "Could you just drop it all?"

"Not likely," Angel said. "But Tia's not Melissa, and I'm not you."

Will stared at the drip-stained floor, running Angel's words through his mind. He made it sound so simple, but Will's breaking up with Melissa would be the hardest conversation of his life. Just the thought made him sick to his stomach.

Angel pushed himself off the stool and walked over to lean next to Will.

"All I know is, you have to break up with Melissa or clear Jessica's name or apologize to her or something," Angel said firmly. "Because if you don't make a move soon, you're going to lose it— big time."

Angel walked over to a workbench and started sorting through a pile of nuts and bolts. He'd said his piece. Will tucked his chin and let out a deep sigh. Angel was right. If he didn't do something to improve his situation and alleviate his guilt, he was going to explode.

Unfortunately he was slightly more concerned about Melissa doing that very thing.

# Jeremy Aames

In fifth grade I had perfect attendance.

In sixth grade I won the district science fair with my laser project.

In seventh grade I was the star basketball player, and in eighth grade I won the "good citizenship" award that the school gives out annually.

As a freshman, I was the youngest starter in the football lineup, and by my sophomore year, I was a first-string wide receiver, the only sophomore on varsity basketball, and one of the top-ten students in my class.

Junior year I made captain of the football team and managed to maintain a 3.8 GPA. And now, as a senior, I'm still playing ball, inspiring my team, working double shifts, and keeping up my grades.

According to my guidance counselor,

*I'm a shoo-in for three or four different scholarships, and I should be able to attend almost any college I choose. My buddies see me as the one who has it all together, and there are actually underclassmen who look up to me. My teachers love me, my friends' parents all want to adopt me, and Jessica might actually like me.*

*So why do I feel like such a failure?*

# CHAPTER 5
## The Big Letdown

Shot of espresso, steamed milk, sprinkle of cocoa, chocolate syrup, and a dollop of whipped cream.

This had to be the hundredth mochaccino Jeremy had made in the last hour. It was a Monday night, but the artsy theater across the street from House of Java had just let out, and the place was packed. There had been a solid stream of customers for nearly forty-five minutes now, and Jeremy was beginning to wonder if he could develop carpal-tunnel syndrome from working the espresso machine too much.

Finally there seemed to be a break coming. Jeremy served up the coffee with a slice of marble cheesecake, made change, and then paused for breath. Placing both of his hands on the counter, he let his head drop while he stretched out his calves and tried to relax his shoulders. He had been so intent on serving the barrage of customers that he hadn't noticed how tense he was. Football practice had been especially tough—his little inspirational speech seemed to have affected

Coach Anderson too—and now all of his muscles were feeling it.

Jeremy stood up straight, closed his eyes, and slowly let his head roll from side to side. But just as he locked his hands behind his back and started pulling downward to stretch out his chest, he heard the door open.

*Here we go again.*

Jeremy plastered a smile on his face. But when he looked up, no one was there. He leaned over the counter and checked around. None of the people in the café looked like they had just come in.

"Rough night?" he heard from behind. He whirled around to see Jessica standing in front of the espresso machine. She already had a mug in her hand.

"Never sneak up on a person who's had three cappuccinos in one hour," Jeremy said.

"Little jittery, are we?" Jessica asked.

Jessica took a step closer, and Jeremy felt his heart speed up. Was she getting ready to give him a hug, or was that just his wishful thinking? Jessica set down her mug and walked around to the other side of the counter. She pulled up a stool right in front of him and sat down.

"Why don't you pour me some coffee and tell me about it," she suggested, staring at him with her gorgeous aqua eyes.

At that moment he was so glad she was there

that he could have leaned over the counter and kissed her.

"Name your poison," he said with a smile, raising the mug in front of her. "Just don't ask for a mochaccino. I've made one too many of those today."

Jessica grinned. "Don't worry. I just want a simple decaf with cream and a sprinkle of cocoa, please."

Jeremy prepared Jessica's order in a matter of seconds and placed the mug on a napkin in front of her. Then he grabbed the stool next to Jessica and lifted it over the counter, setting it down opposite her and taking a seat.

"So, what made today such a rough day?" Jessica asked, looking up at him through her lashes as she sipped at her coffee.

Jeremy was so lost in her curious and concerned eyes, he forgot to speak. All he could think of was that she must have stopped by to see him. She wasn't working. She wasn't with friends. So she had to be here to see him. Unreal.

"You know," he answered finally, "suddenly my day doesn't seem so important. But there is something else I'd like to talk to you about."

Jessica's posture stiffened.

"It's nothing bad," Jeremy added hurriedly. "I was just wondering . . . There's this party on Friday night, and I thought maybe you'd like to go."

Jessica blinked.

"With me," Jeremy finished uncertainly. Jeremy saw a small smile start to play on Jessica's lips, but it was gone so quickly, he was left wondering if he'd imagined it. The spark in her eyes seemed to fizzle, and she suddenly seemed strangely distant.

*I read her wrong,* Jeremy thought, a sickening feeling seeping into his heart. *She's not remotely interested.* Part of him wanted to just disappear into the back room, but he didn't want to look like a total loser. He had to stay and stick out his rejection like a man.

"Jess?" he prompted, searching her face.

"Sorry," she responded, laughing nervously and sitting up straight. "I guess I'm a little tired tonight."

She ran one hand through her fine, blond hair and stared down into her coffee mug as though something inside it had piqued her interest.

"That sounds fun," she said finally, "but I'm not sure I can this weekend." Her eyes remained lowered as she spoke.

"Oh. Okay. I didn't . . . I mean, I didn't want to put you on the spot or anything," he said quickly. "I just thought it might be nice for us to see each other out of these green aprons for a change." Jeremy tugged at the string around his neck playfully, hoping he was being charming rather than pathetic.

Jessica finally looked up at him, an almost timid look on her face.

"It would," she said quietly. "Sometime."

To Maria's surprise, Ken was already in his seat when she walked into history class on Tuesday morning. She made a beeline for his desk and dropped her things loudly on top of it to get his attention.

"You're about eighteen hours late," Maria said.

Ken reluctantly raised his head and gave her his patented blank stare.

Maria looked at her watch and then held it up to her ear as if it might not be working. "And you're also supposed to be in the library, I think."

Ken sighed and slumped a bit lower in his chair. His normally shorn blond hair was getting rather long in the back, and his bangs hung down carelessly, almost obscuring one eye. Too short to look intentional and too long to look stylish. His denim jacket was sporting serious grass stains, his hands were blistered, and his nails were grubby. The smell of cut grass hung around him like a vapor cloud.

"What did you do while I was sitting alone in the library? Wrestle cows?" Maria asked, leaning over his desk so he couldn't possibly ignore her.

Ken rolled his eyes and looked off to the side, exhaling sharply.

"Pigs, actually," he said sarcastically.

What was with this guy? He couldn't possibly be the same Ken Matthews who used to throw passes to Aaron Dallas down crowded corridors over the heads of giggling freshman girls who idolized him.

Maria realized she was staring at him with a mixture of pity and disbelief. She snapped herself out of it.

"I waited in the library for you for over an hour."

Ken sat silently, staring off into space. Maria knew he just wanted her to shut up and go away, but she wasn't about to let it go that easily.

"Look, Ken. I know you aren't particularly concerned with your grades, but you're not the only one involved here. My grade is on the line too, in case you hadn't noticed. We're supposed to be working together."

Ken turned to face her with a look so distant and devoid of emotion that it almost frightened her. "Back off, Maria. Just go ahead and do whatever you want on this stupid project, but don't expect any help from me." If his tone had been harsher, the words would have stung, but in his droning monotone, it was almost depressing. How was she supposed to draw out someone who didn't want to be drawn out?

"Fine," Maria said crisply, picking up her bag

and turning away. She took a seat two rows ahead of him so she wouldn't have to see his face during class. What a jerk. But what had she expected anyway? She had known working with Ken wasn't exactly going to be easy.

*Oh, well,* she thought, pulling out her notebook and pen just as the bell rang. *At least if I'm working on my own, I know everything will get done right.*

Elizabeth leaned on the flagpole in front of Sweet Valley High, waiting for her chronically late sister to materialize. Today was her day to relinquish the Jeep to Jessica, but she needed her sister to drive her home first—home to the Sandborns'.

Jessica had cheerleading practice, so Elizabeth had spent the last hour hanging around the *Oracle* office working on her piece for that week's paper and feeling decidedly uncomfortable. She was the editor in chief of the school weekly, but she'd been skipping a lot of meetings lately. One younger staff member had even asked her who she was. Elizabeth was so embarrassed, she had finished up quickly and bolted. Now all she wanted to do was get back to the Sandborns' and veg.

"Don't move, Liz; the flagpole might fall down," she heard a voice call.

"Very funny," she said, turning to face Conner. His voice was unmistakable. There was always that underlying tone of sarcasm that betrayed him.

"What are you still doing here?" she asked, infinitely pleased to hear herself speaking to him in a tone that wasn't a bit nervous or flirtatious.

"I could ask you the same question, but I bet I already know," he said. "Another tireless day at the *Oracle* for Lois Lane?" He chuckled a little, obviously amused with himself.

"Actually, no," she lied, not wanting to give him an inch. "I had a physics lab to finish up after school. You might want to get your X-ray vision checked out."

"Are you implying that I'm Superman?"

"There you go, pairing us up again," Elizabeth said, beating him to the punch. But Conner looked puzzled. Elizabeth bit her tongue.

"I was kidding," she said hurriedly. "You know, that first time we talked in the library . . . You called me Barbie, and I called you Ken, and then you accused me of making us into a couple?" She was trying to jog his memory, but she couldn't help feeling like she was just digging herself into an increasingly large hole.

"You're getting too quick for me, Liz. I'm gonna have to start watching myself around you."

The front door to the school opened and Elizabeth glanced over, but it wasn't Jessica. She checked her watch and sighed.

"Expecting someone?" Conner asked. For a

moment Elizabeth entertained the thought that maybe he actually cared who she was meeting. Maybe she should pretend she was meeting a guy just to see what Conner's reaction would be.

But Elizabeth wasn't a game player, and she didn't think Conner was either. At least, not at heart.

"I'm waiting for Jessica. She's supposed to give me a ride home—I mean to your house—so she can have the Jeep tonight." To her surprise, Conner didn't seize on the fact that she had referred to his house as "home."

"Don't make her drive the extra miles," Conner said. "I'm headed that way now if you want a ride."

"Sure," Elizabeth said evenly. Alone time with Conner was often agonizing, but never dull. "Let me just leave a note on the Jeep for her. Where are you parked?" Conner pointed over at the corner of the parking lot, and Elizabeth nodded.

"Okay. I'll meet you at your car," she said.

Elizabeth walked over to the Jeep and scribbled a quick note to her sister. Then she took a deep breath, straightened her skirt, and reminded herself to remain calm.

Yes, she was going to be alone in the car for twenty minutes with Conner, and yes, she had been doing well so far, but she knew that she could easily screw it all up in a matter of moments.

As Elizabeth approached Conner's car, he leaned over and popped the door for her.

"Thanks," Elizabeth said, not bothering to cover up her surprise at the gesture. She set her book bag on the floor as she climbed in, immediately reaching up for her seat belt. Once she had it buckled, she pulled down on the bottom of her blue V-necked shirt to straighten it out and then shifted in her seat a few times to get comfortable. Finally she shook her head, tucked a stray strand of hair behind her ear, and looked over at Conner. The amused glint in his eyes told her he'd been watching her the whole time.

"If you're done primping, we can leave now," he said, grinning. Elizabeth felt her face getting hot.

"All set," she managed in a surprisingly steady voice. Conner stared at her a little longer. His smirk turned into a full-fledged smile so rare that it almost made Elizabeth sigh aloud.

When he smiled like that, it was almost impossible for her to look away.

"Good night, Jeremy," Mr. Aames said as he passed by his son's bedroom door.

"Night, Dad," Jeremy responded, meeting his father's tired eyes briefly. As Mr. Aames continued down the hallway to his own bedroom, Jeremy realized that "good night" and "good morning" were the only words he and his father had exchanged over the past three days. And things hadn't been any better with his mother. Jeremy was beginning to wonder how much longer the three of them could go on living together without communicating. At least his sisters were noisy.

It was nine-thirty, and Jeremy was sitting in his bedroom, poring over his history notes. He had a big test tomorrow morning, and even though history was his strongest subject, he felt compelled to go over everything just one more time.

"Oh, so dedicated," Jeremy muttered to the empty room. "We'll see how much longer that lasts."

The phone rang, startling Jeremy from his thoughts. He reached over to the corner of his desk and picked up the receiver immediately, hoping to get it before the ringing disturbed his parents.

"Hello?"

"Jeremy, great. I'm not calling too late, am I?"

"No, it's fine," Jeremy responded, not quite sure who he had on the other end of the line.

"Good. Look, Corey had to cancel for her shift tomorrow afternoon, so I was wondering if you could cover it." Finally recognition set in. It was Ally.

"Sure. What time?" he asked.

"I'll need you from right after school until about six-thirty." Jeremy winced. Right after school? That would mean cutting football practice.

"Oh, I'm sorry, Ally, I can't," he said with true regret. He would have liked the extra hours. "I have practice. What if I show up at four? Would that help?"

Ally sighed. "Four's no good. I need someone earlier. Look, Jeremy, you're the one who wanted more hours," she reminded him.

"I know, I know," he responded, stalling for time to think it over. Maybe there was some way to work it out. He really needed the money. But skipping football practice . . . How could he? How would it look to the rest of the team if the captain cut practice to work? It wasn't exactly the kind of thing that inspired loyalty and team unity. Then again, it would only be this once. Coach Anderson and the rest of the team would understand, wouldn't they?

"Jeremy," Ally's irritated voice said. "I need an answer. What'll it be? Can you do it, or should I call someone else?"

"I can work," Jeremy answered hesitantly.

"You sure?"

"Yeah. No problem. I'll be there right after school."

"Great. Talk to you later."

When Jeremy hung up the phone, he was instantly sure he'd done the wrong thing.

He flipped through his history book and tried

to concentrate on the United States's reasons for entering World War II. But his mind was racing. Images flashed in front of his eyes. Running laps. Spilling coffee. Taking a test. Playing with Trisha. Mowing the lawn. Fixing a leaky sink. Catching a pass. Pouring more coffee. His father's tired eyes. Ally, Trent, Jessica, Coach, his mom.

Jeremy folded his arms on his desk and dropped his head. All the muddled, flashing thoughts added up to one clear conclusion.

No matter what he did, he was letting somebody down.

# TIA RAMIREZ

From: tee@swiftnet.com
To: mcdermott@cal.rr.com
Time:7:28 P.M.
Subject:where are you?!!!

hey, c! what's up?!!

you left andy's early on saturday, blew us off for the movie saturday night, ran out on us at hoj sunday morning (ok, so I know why you left that time—but still!), ditched us at andy's on monday, and disappeared after school tuesday.

what gives? stress at home or something? andy, angel, and i are starting to feel neglected, and i'm beginning to think you found another flavor of the week you haven't told me about yet . . . hmmm?

whatever.

call me (if you can find the time!)
—tee

Maria hastily grabbed a cocktail napkin from the table she was about to scrub down and collected her tip. Two dollars.

"Wow. Nice tip," Jade Wu, one of Maria's fellow waitresses, said sarcastically as she walked by.

"Seriously," Maria answered, shoving the money in her apron pocket. "I'll have to thank those people for contributing to my college fund."

"Look at this place," Jade said, gesturing at the nearly empty dining area of First and Ten. "I skipped out of cheerleading practice early for this?"

"Yeah. Wednesday afternoons are pretty useless," Maria said. "But the tips on Fridays and Saturdays make it worth it."

"I guess," Jade said with a slight shrug.

"Hey, girls!" Ted Wiley, the bartender, signaled to Maria and Jade from across the room. "One of you wanna come over here and pick up these plates?" There were a few used place settings on the bar that the busboy had obviously ignored.

"I'll go if you bring these glasses to the kitchen," Maria offered.

"Deal," Jade said, picking up Maria's full tray. "I think I'll take a nap while I'm back there."

Maria laughed. "Good call."

"How's it goin', Slater?" Ted asked as Maria walked over to the bar. She placed Jade's tray on the counter, and Ted started to load it up with dishes.

"Okay," Maria answered. "I'm pretty bored."

Ted ran a hand over his balding head and smiled. "Me too. I'd probably be countin' beer nuts right now if it wasn't for this guy." Ted nodded toward the tables, and Maria turned around to check out his one customer.

It was Ken Matthews. He was slouched in a chair, nursing a Coke, staring at one of First and Ten's many televisions.

"Oh, great," Maria muttered.

"You know him?" Ted asked.

"Yeah, and I'd like to dump this Sprite over his head," Maria grumbled. So Ken was too busy to work on their history project, but he could find time to watch ESPN? She'd give him something to watch. Maria started toward him, determined to give him another lecture on why he damn well better start pulling his weight.

"Hey," Ted said, grabbing her wrist. "I don't know what the guy did, but take it easy on him.

He looks like he just found out his mama died."

Maria paused and glanced at Ken. Ted was right. Ken looked *so* sad, staring sullenly at the screen. Was this how he spent all his afternoons? Sitting alone in front of a television somewhere, blocking out the rest of the world?

"Don't worry, Ted. I'll go easy on him," Maria said.

She took a deep breath, slowly strolled over to Ken's table, and pulled out a chair.

"Mind if I sit down?" she asked. Ken didn't even look at her. He just shrugged and continued to stare at the TV. Maria perched on the chair and checked the program. Some guy was sitting at a desk, spouting off NFL statistics.

"What are you watching?" Maria asked. Ken took a gulp of his soda and set it down heavily.

"SportsCenter," he said plainly. Maria nodded and pretended to be interested. He'd said two words without telling her to get lost. That was a start.

"I'm surprised you're still interested in football," she said. "I mean, you quit the team and everything." Ken didn't respond. "Do you ever think about going back?"

Ken stared up at the ceiling for a moment, obviously aggravated, and then closed his eyes altogether. The expression on his face was so cold, so full of resentment, that Maria actually recoiled.

"Don't you have tables to clean or something?" He never even looked at her.

"Don't worry about my job—"

"I'm *not* worried about your job," Ken snapped, finally turning to look at her. His blue eyes were devoid of emotion, but his tone was biting. "Can't you take a hint? I want you out of my face."

"Hey, you," Jeremy called as Jessica swung open the large front door at House of Java and glided into the room. She flashed the irresistible smile that always made Jeremy want to grab her and kiss her on the spot. Of course, considering the semi–shoot down she'd dished out the other day, a kiss was out of the question.

"I'm just gonna put my stuff in back," she called as she made her way around the counter.

*Incredible,* Jeremy thought as he finished wiping down the table he was working on. She hadn't passed within five feet of him, and yet Jeremy could feel the warmth radiating from her.

"Didya ask her out yet?" Jeremy's coworker, Daniel Hannigan, asked from behind the counter.

"Sort of," Jeremy said, trying to duck the question.

"Sort of?" Daniel said with a laugh. "Got shot down, huh?"

"Not quite," Jeremy hedged, slinging the rag over his shoulder.

"Sort of and not quite," Daniel repeated. He leaned against the counter as Jeremy came over and threw the rag down in front of him.

"It was a non-straight-answer type of thing," Jeremy admitted. He climbed up onto a stool and rested his elbows on the countertop. "Maybe she's just shy."

Daniel laughed and adjusted his battered Dodgers baseball cap. "Yeah, she's shy," he said. "And we serve only decaffeinated beverages."

Jeremy smirked but felt his spirits droop. "You think I should give up?" he asked.

"No way, dude," Daniel said, slapping Jeremy on the shoulder. "That babe's worth all kinds of humiliation and groveling. I'd at least give it a second try."

Jessica pushed through the back-room door and joined Daniel behind the counter. "Give what a second try?" she asked.

Jeremy shot Daniel a panicked look.

"The SATs," Daniel blurted out, grinning. "Jeremy crashed and burned."

"No, I didn't," Jeremy objected, reddening.

"Don't be ashamed, my man," Daniel said. "It's a lot of pressure. Not everyone can remember how to spell their name under those conditions."

"You misspelled your name?" Jessica asked incredulously. Jeremy made a mental note to devise some cruel and unusual punishment for Daniel.

"Well, gotta go," Daniel said, untying his apron. "You two kids have fun." He shot Jeremy one more amused glance before disappearing into the back room.

"He's kidding, right?" Jessica said, straightening the cups that held the stirrers and spoons.

"Yes. He's kidding," Jeremy said wearily.

Jessica narrowed her eyes. She grabbed a straw from the dispenser and started chewing on the end. "Another rough day?"

"Not at all," Jeremy said, scratching at the back of his neck. "I actually had a pretty good day, considering that I'm three chapters behind in *Crime and Punishment* and I still managed a B-plus on my quiz."

Jessica raised her eyebrows.

"I'm impressed. Not bad for a jock who can't spell his name," she teased, her blue-green eyes sparkling mischievously.

Jeremy snagged his rag from the counter and tossed it at Jessica. She caught it easily and whipped it back at him, hitting him square on the chest.

"Not bad for a cheerleader," Jeremy shot back, grinning at her sideways. Jessica laughed and tossed her straw into the garbage can behind her. She took a napkin from the pile next to the register and leaned over the counter, tugging at his apron where the cloth had hit him.

"I think I owe it to you to wipe this off." She dabbed at Jeremy's shirt and apron with a napkin, leaning so close that he could smell her hair. If he leaned down just a bit, he could brush his lips against her head, but Jeremy forced himself to stand still.

"Hey, Jess," he said softly. She stopped what she was doing and looked up at him, their faces inches apart. Jeremy swallowed hard.

"I was wondering . . . did you give any more thought to the idea of going to that party with me on Friday night?" Jessica pulled back and crumpled up the napkin. Jeremy knew he had caught her off guard again. She started to speak, but Jeremy beat her to it.

"Listen, it's at my best friend's house and he dates a girl from another school, so it's not like you'd be the only one there who wasn't from Big Mesa—"

"That's not it—"

"And I'll introduce you to everybody. I'm sure you'd like my friends, and I know they'd like you. But if you felt uncomfortable, we could leave. We could go grab a burger or see a movie or something. . . ."

Jeremy heard himself babbling and trailed off. One word was repeating itself over and over in his mind. *Lame, lame, lame.*

Jessica was looking down, slowly shredding the

napkin and making a little pile of paper droppings on the counter. So much for easing into it.

"I'd really like to," Jessica said without looking up. Jeremy knew that tone of voice. He was about to be let down gently—again. "But I have a project due on Monday that's going to take most of my time this weekend." She looked up at him with what appeared to be regret in her eyes. "I'm really sorry."

*Great,* Jeremy thought. *Turned down for home-work.* She might as well have said she had to stay home and wash her hair. That was one of the lamest excuses he had ever heard. She obviously didn't like him. Except as a friend, of course, which was just one step above being detested.

"Hey, it's cool," he said, trying to retreat with a shred of dignity. He looked down at his apron and laughed halfheartedly. "Spot's gone. You did a good job of cleaning me up." As hard as he tried, he couldn't seem to banish the disappointment from his voice. The worst part was that Jessica was looking at him like he was a stray dog that she couldn't find a home for. He started to turn away to scrub down some more tables, but Jessica touched his hand gently.

"I know it sounds lame," she said, her eyes pleading, "but I really do have a big project to do." Jeremy smiled weakly, and Jessica continued. "Seriously—it's been driving me crazy all week.

It's for drama class, and I just can't figure out where to start."

"What's the assignment?" Jeremy ventured, hoping there was one. Jessica rolled her eyes and groaned.

"I'm supposed to cut up magazines and stuff and make a collage that illustrates who I really am."

"Who you really are?" Jeremy repeated.

"Yeah, I know, it sounds stupid. My drama teacher's going all existential on me," Jessica said, smiling slightly. "Anyway, I've been going through stuff for five nights now, and I just can't figure out what to do."

Jeremy wondered why a project like that would give someone like Jessica any trouble. She had so many great qualities that he knew he could do it in a snap. In fact, Jeremy was pretty sure he could wallpaper a room with clippings about Jessica's positive traits.

But there was no sense pushing the issue now. She had said no, and he needed to drop it—not make her feel like she had to defend herself or make himself look like a total loser.

"Yeah, that doesn't sound like fun," he sympathized. Jessica gave him a thin smile, and he knew she was relieved he wasn't going to pursue the subject any further.

"So, should I show you how to make an iced Frappuccino today?" Jeremy asked, forcing levity.

"Why don't I show you?" she countered, a glint in her eye. "I worked with Ally on Tuesday, and I am now an iced-drink expert."

"Well, then, be my guest, guru," Jeremy said.

He walked back around the counter as Jessica grabbed a tall mug and some ice. She confidently took him through all the steps as she made the drink, never looking to him for help or approval.

Jeremy shook his head and sighed. He had to admire her ability to move past an awkward moment so easily. Unfortunately he just wanted to crawl under a table and die.

*Stupid, stupid, stupid,* Elizabeth admonished herself. *I should never drink grape juice when I'm wearing white.*

While reaching for a pencil on her desk, Elizabeth had managed to jostle her glass just enough to splash grape juice on her shirt, leaving a large purple stain on the front. It was one of her favorites—a cotton button-down with a flared collar and French cuffs—and it was white, so there wasn't much chance of covering up the stain if she didn't get it out right away.

Throwing on an old gray T-shirt, Elizabeth sprinted down the stairs to the laundry room. With a little bleach and some cold water, she just might be able to save the shirt. She dashed across the cool cement of the basement floor, barely even registering the fact that Conner was sitting on a table, leaning back against the wall.

"Major laundry emergency?" he asked. Elizabeth splashed a few drops of bleach into the washing machine and then turned to face Conner, who appeared mildly amused.

"Something like that. I spilled juice all over my shirt, and I don't particularly want it to leave a big stain." She eyed Conner's outfit admiringly. Tattered jeans, worn white tee. "You could probably pull it off, but the grunge look doesn't suit me quite as well."

Elizabeth worked some detergent into the stain and tossed the shirt into the washing machine. She flicked the dial and turned back to Conner.

"So, what are you doing hiding out down here anyway?" She leaned back against the washer, mildly aware of the loud whirring noise it made as it filled with water.

"Even we grungy types have to do our laundry sooner or later," he returned, gesturing at the dryer, which was also running.

"I didn't mean it that way," she said. "I don't think you're dirty-grungy. I just meant that you can do that wrinkled, tousled, torn-clothing thing and actually look okay."

Conner chuckled.

"Somehow it just doesn't work on me," Elizabeth added.

"Never know till you give it a try," Conner said, returning his focus to the book in his hand. *Why does everything he says sound suggestive?* Elizabeth wondered. Was it his low, gravelly voice, or was it her overactive imagination that seemed to kick into high gear whenever she was around Conner? Probably a little of both.

Elizabeth studied the book Conner was reading. She couldn't make out the title, but she could see that it was something by Louis L'Amour. She sighed out loud, causing Conner to look up again.

"Sorry," she said. "I was just looking at your book. How can you read westerns?"

Conner laughed quietly. He folded over the corner of a page, closed the book, and set it down next to him. He pulled himself forward on the table so that his legs hung down, his feet almost touching the floor.

"Ever read one?" he asked, narrowing his eyes and staring at her accusingly. Elizabeth shifted her weight from one side to the other and folded her arms across her chest.

"Well, no, but—"

"All right, then," he said, holding up his index finger. "Let me tell you why the great American western deserves a lot more credit than it gets." Conner's deep green eyes were intense, and his lips were twisted into the smirk that Elizabeth had come to know meant she was about to be put in her place. At least that's what Conner thought. Elizabeth exhaled loudly, keeping her arms folded but allowing her posture to relax slightly. She was ready this time.

"Go ahead. Convince me," she challenged him. She had learned that Conner wasn't one to back down from a good debate. In fact, he actually seemed to enjoy arguing with her.

"First of all, a good western has a tone and style that separate it from other genres of literature. From page one you can almost hear the twangy guitar in the background, spurs jangling, boot heels clicking on dry, wooden saloon floors. The description is incredible, and if an author is good, like Louis here"—Conner wagged his beat-up book at Elizabeth—"even a nondrinker will be thirsty for a belt of whiskey by the end of the first chapter."

"Oookay." Elizabeth tilted her head and looked at him skeptically. She'd never heard him say so many words at one time. He seemed to realize this at the exact moment she did.

"You know what?" he said. "Forget it." He leaned back again and picked up his book.

"No, really," Elizabeth implored, amused by his sensitivity on the subject. "I want to hear more about how I too can learn to love whiskey." Elizabeth snorted a laugh. "I mean, that must be some serious writing."

Conner looked up at her and half-smiled.

*Score one for me,* she thought.

"Speaking of writing, what are you working on for Quigley's class?" Conner asked. Elizabeth was startled by the sudden change of topic. She looked away quickly, hoping he wouldn't see her blush. Ever since Saturday, all Elizabeth had been able to eke out was bad poetry about Conner. He'd have a field day with that one.

"Nothing much," she muttered. "Nothing at all, really. I mean, I just started it, so I'm not sure where it's going." Conner leaned forward, his gaze roaming over Elizabeth suspiciously. Elizabeth tried not to notice, but she knew he was wondering why she had dodged his question.

"Come on, Liz. It's just shoptalk," he prodded.

"Really, it's nothing," Elizabeth insisted. She looked up at the ceiling as Conner moved even closer.

"You're going to have to read it aloud in class on Friday, you know," he persisted. "You might as well tell me now."

Her body temperature rose about ten degrees every time he inched closer. Was she the only one who could feel it? Did he even remember their kiss? She couldn't take it anymore. She couldn't handle being this close to him and remembering what it had felt like to kiss him and knowing she'd never get up the guts to do it again.

Elizabeth took a step back as if she could move

away from whatever force field Conner had her suspended in.

"Sorry. You'll just have to wait and hear it with everyone else," she told him, managing a smirk of her own. His interest was actually amusing . . . when she got past the fact that it was also totally intriguing. Conner gave her one last searching look, then shrugged. He pushed himself off the table and walked over to the now quiet dryer.

"Oh, well," he said, taking out a pair of faded jeans and folding them. "It's probably some kind of 'Save the Whales' essay or something anyway."

"Just wait," Elizabeth said coyly. "You might be surprised." She opened the washer to check on the progress of her shirt, aware of Conner's eyes following her every move.

Elizabeth smiled to herself. If she wasn't mistaken, she wasn't the only one who was intrigued.

Jeremy sat down heavily on the brown leather sofa in his family's living room. He let himself sink back into the soft, smooth upholstery, putting his feet up on the cherry-wood, mission-style coffee table in front of him.

His mother had sold most of the family's furniture in a quiet estate sale a few months ago, but Jeremy was glad she'd held on to a few of the more comfortable things . . . especially the big-screen TV.

Jeremy was tempted to zone out to whatever

late-night talk show he could find, but the remote was nowhere in sight, and he didn't feel like looking for it. Every muscle in his body ached.

It had been another long day. He'd arrived at school early to run laps, having decided that if he was going to miss football practice, he'd better show up both Wednesday and Thursday morning to make up for it. He didn't want Coach Anderson or any of his teammates to think he was slacking off. Then after school he had gone immediately to House of Java for a double shift. Of course, the first part had flown by because Jessica had worked with him until eight—

Jessica. What was going on there? Jeremy knew where things stood from his perspective—he was falling for her. But he couldn't figure out what she thought of him. One minute she seemed to like him too, and the next she was blowing him off. And that project. Why would she have trouble with something like that? Was it just an excuse?

Jeremy put his feet down on the floor and leaned forward, rubbing his eyes. It was a good thing he had gotten most of his homework done in study hall because all he felt like doing at the moment was going to bed. He opened his eyes and glanced at the magazines on top of the coffee table. One of the headlines made him pause. It read: "The Woman Who Does it All."

Jeremy started flipping through the stack of

magazines on the table. They were old ones that his mom had been meaning to throw out for a long time, but instead they just kept piling up. As Jeremy scanned the pages, a thousand things jumped out at him. "A Powerful Force" from an ad for a new SUV and "Sweetly Seductive" from something about perfume. "Delicate" and "honest" from various articles and "a roller-coaster ride of excitement" from a section of book reviews.

Suddenly energized, Jeremy ran up to his room and returned with a piece of bright blue poster board, scissors, and a glue stick. He started cutting and pasting like a madman. Describing Jessica like this was even easier than he had thought it would be.

He was almost finished with the collage when his mother walked in. She was wearing her bathrobe and slippers and appeared tired and worn as usual.

"I thought I heard you down here," she said, taking a seat on the arm of the sofa. "What are you working on?"

"Just a project for school," Jeremy answered. He watched while his mother scrutinized the poster in front of him, squinting as her eyes fell on phrases like, "A True Femme Fatale" and "The Girl Next Door."

"Remind me to ask you about this when I'm more awake," she said, patting him on the back.

Jeremy grinned and nodded. "Anyway, let's talk about this house thing. I'd like to explain."

"You don't have to," Jeremy jumped in. "I'm sorry about the other night. I mean, I still don't want to move, but I understand why you think we have to."

Jeremy's mother slid down onto the sofa, resting on the cushion next to his.

"That's only part of it, though, Jeremy," she said. "It's true that we can't afford it—the upkeep is just too expensive—and that is the primary reason we need to sell it, but it's also your father."

"What do you mean?" Jeremy asked.

"Well, he just seems to be stuck, like he's treading water or something. He won't go to your uncle for help, and he won't take a job that he considers beneath himself. The longer he stays like this—just stagnant—the worse he gets." She sighed. "Maybe a move to a smaller place will shock him out of his stupor. It could be a good thing for all of us."

Jeremy knew his mother was right. His father hadn't been trying very hard to improve things. It was almost as if he had given up hope altogether.

"I know, Mom," he said, forcing a weak smile. "You're right. Moving is probably the best thing for all of us right now." He watched as his mother's expression visibly relaxed. At least he had been able to take away one of her worries: Her son didn't hate her, and he understood. Maybe now she'd be able to get some sleep.

As if reading his thoughts, Mrs. Aames stood up and covered a yawn with her hand.

"I think I'm going to head back upstairs," she said, stretching. "It's almost midnight. You shouldn't stay up much longer yourself."

"Yeah, I'm almost done here. I'll be right up too," Jeremy said. His mother leaned down and kissed him on the cheek.

"Everything's going to work out, you know," she told him, but Jeremy couldn't help feeling that her words lacked conviction.

"I know, Mom," he said, nodding in agreement. But as she turned to go, Jeremy stopped her. "Let me know if there's anything I can do. Okay?" Jeremy's mother smiled, but her eyes were full of guilt. She shook her head and gave him a purely maternal look.

"Jeremy, my dear, you already do far too much." Jeremy smiled and let his mother go, but in his head, her words were drowned out by his own cynical voice.

*Yeah, but it's still not enough.*

# Jessica Wakefield

## Great Things That Have Happened to Me Lately That I, of Course, Managed to Turn Bad

1. Jeremy somehow made it past Melissa and Lila without hearing what a "slut" I am. (Unfortunately that means I ditched the first game of the year for no good reason.)

2. Elizabeth gave up her job at HOJ so that I could work there. (Unfortunately the main reason I wanted to work there was Jeremy, and I think I've now officially alienated him. See 4 and 5.)

3. I made my first triple half-caf, nonfat,

sugarless latte. (Unfortunately the customer burned her tongue and threatened to sue.)

4. Jeremy asked me out. (Unfortunately I turned him down because I'm such a wuss, I'm afraid to go out in public.)

5. Jeremy asked me out again. (Unfortunately I turned him down again, this time because I had too much homework to do. I'm such a geek now.)

Remind me that the next time something good happens (if it ever does), I have to just enjoy it.

# Elizabeth Wakefield

She was afraid to look at him
Because he might recognize
The love, longing, and secrecy
Betrayed within her eyes.

Aaaaaaaghhhh! I'm never going to get this right! It's hard enough trying to express my feelings about Conner without sounding all sappy and sentimental, but now I can't stop rhyming!

I need something else to write about.

I need to get him out of my head before I become totally talentless.

I need a life.

# I Am the Geek

**7**

"You are so lucky you don't have to live at the Fowlers' anymore," Jessica said, leaning her elbows on the kitchen table. "Thank you so much for inviting me over here."

Elizabeth placed a tub of pseudo-butter down on the table. "You can have breakfast here anytime," she said, grabbing a seat next to her sister. "I completely understand the need to escape Lila."

"It's not just her," Jessica said with a sigh. "Mom and Dad are keeping more to themselves than ever, and I spend most of my time either hidden in my room studying or trying to smuggle in a pint of Ben & Jerry's without being reprimanded by the kitchen staff."

Elizabeth laughed as she poured out two glasses of orange juice. "It's so different from home."

"So true," Jessica said wryly, chomping on a piece of toast.

"At least you get to *see* Mom and Dad. I couldn't believe it when they had to cancel our weekly dinner last weekend," Elizabeth said. "Talking to them on the phone is weird. It's like I'm already at college or something."

"You could come over once in a while," Jessica pointed out.

Elizabeth felt her face grow warm. Major guilt. "I know. I'll try to be better about it. I just feel like I'm always busy." She paused and smiled at her sister. "Let's make a promise to do this breakfast thing more often. And next time we'll have it at your place."

"Deal," Jessica said, holding out her half-eaten piece of toast. Elizabeth "clicked" her cereal spoon against Jessica's bread.

"God. I'd give just about anything to be back in our old house right now," Jessica said. "Do you know how long it's been since we had Dad's blueberry pancakes?"

Elizabeth stared at her soggy cereal. "Thanks for reminding me," she said. "Have Mom and Dad said anything new about rebuilding?"

Jessica shook her head. "Not really. I mean, they have a contractor and everything, but Dad said he's still waiting for something to come through on the insurance."

"I wish I understood all that stuff," Elizabeth said. She finished off her juice and leaned back in her chair.

"Don't even try," Jessica said, gulping her own

juice down. "So, how are things here? Do you like it?" She paused and looked around. "Where are they all anyway? It's Thursday morning, and this place is deserted."

"Yeah, well, Megan goes running with the soccer team some mornings, and I never really know what Conner's doing."

*Or thinking or feeling,* she said to herself.

"He's probably still in bed," she added, looking up at the ceiling as though she could see through to Conner's room.

"What about Mrs. Sandborn?" Jessica asked, helping herself to a nearly overflowing bowl of cereal. "Doesn't she work or anything?"

"She does charity work and stuff. Sporadically, I think." Elizabeth paused for a moment. "You know, it's weird. I never really see her. She always seems to stay out late and get up after we've all left for school. I'm not really sure where she spends all her time."

Jessica leaned closer to her sister. "Maybe she's a secret agent, and if she told you where she went all the time, she'd have to kill you," she whispered, her eyes wide.

Elizabeth elbowed Jessica on the arm. "You're such a geek," she jibed.

Jessica laughed, but gradually her face started to fall. She placed her spoon down on the table and swallowed with obvious difficulty. "Oh my God, you're right."

Elizabeth laughed. "Shut up, Jess. You're so melodramatic." She stood up and started clearing her dishes to the sink.

"No! I'm totally serious!" Jessica said, staring straight ahead. "I *am* the geek. For the first time in our lives, I'm the geek and you're . . . not."

Elizabeth put her dishes back down on the table. "Okay, you'd better explain that one. Quick."

"Seriously, think about it," Jessica said, turning around in her seat to face Elizabeth. "All I do anymore is study because I have nothing else to do, and you must spend more time out with friends than I do, considering that I don't have any anymore."

Elizabeth's expression softened. "Jess, it's not that bad," she said.

"And I'm stuck at stuffy old Fowler Tomb," Jessica continued, "while you're living here with the hottest guy in the entire school—"

"Excuse me?" Elizabeth said, walking around the counter and reclaiming her seat. "Are you talking about Conner?" She knew people thought Conner was attractive, but the hottest guy in the school? Was he seriously that popular?

"Oh, don't be dense, Liz. You must have noticed by now that over half the female population at SVH wants to date him." Jessica pushed her half-eaten cereal away from her. "I may be a total outcast, but I can still recognize drool when I see it. Everyone thinks he's totally cool, though I don't get it."

Elizabeth's eyebrows shot up. "You don't?" she asked.

"Okay, he's hot. But who could get past that attitude?" Jessica asked. "He has such an obvious ego. Besides, didn't he, like, crush Maria?"

Elizabeth felt her heart twist, and she looked down at the table, hoping Jessica wouldn't notice her blush.

"Yeah, I guess he did," she said finally. "But they were totally incompatible."

"I guess," Jessica said. Elizabeth could hear the suspicion in Jessica's voice.

"What?" she asked, looking up.

"Defending the guy who broke your best friend's heart?" Jessica asked. Elizabeth tried to hold her sister's gaze. If she could manage not to flinch, she had a shot at convincing Jessica she was wrong. But Elizabeth blinked first.

"No way!" Jessica exclaimed, her eyes lighting up. "You like him!"

Elizabeth stood up and grabbed Jessica's bowl and glass.

"No, I don't," she said, turning away from Jessica and walking to the sink. She couldn't talk to her sister about this yet. Not when everything with Conner was so up in the air, when Maria was still walking around devastated, and when Jessica's own life was in the social gutter.

"Are you sure?" Jessica asked, getting up from the table and bringing the rest of her dishes to the sink. "Because you don't usually avoid looking at me unless you have a secret."

Elizabeth turned to face her sister. "I'm not avoiding you," she said, looking Jessica straight in the . . . forehead. "Maybe I do think he's cool, and even good-looking," she conceded. The best way to get around her sister was always to admit to something smaller. "But I just like him as a friend. Besides, I barely know him."

Jessica studied her twin's face for a moment while Elizabeth did her best to look sincere. "All right," Jessica finally said. "I'll back off . . . for now."

Suddenly Conner's stereo blared to life above their heads, and Elizabeth and Jessica both jumped.

"There he is now," Elizabeth said.

Jessica checked her watch and sneered. "What does he do, roll out of bed and into his car?"

"Don't worry, Jess. He showers," Elizabeth said.

"It doesn't show," Jessica answered, eyeing Elizabeth to see if she would defend him. No way was Elizabeth going to fall for that one.

"We'd better get going," she said, running some water into the sink to cover the dishes. "We need to get to school so we can practice our skit for French class today."

"Right. Because now I'm a geek!" Jessica said, grabbing her book bag.

"Exactly!" Elizabeth agreed cheerily. "Besides, if we stay any longer, you might have to deal with Conner."

Jessica picked up her sweater and keys and headed for the foyer. "Then we definitely better get going," she said over her shoulder.

*Definitely,* Elizabeth thought, picking up her own things and rushing after her sister. *Because if Jessica sees me around Conner for two seconds, she'll know I was lying.*

*Library. 3:30. If you don't show, I'm telling Mr. Ford to flunk you.*

Maria glanced up at Mr. Ford, who was lost in his own lecture about the Great Depression. She folded her note into a tiny square and tapped Ken on the shoulder with it. No reaction. She tapped him again, but he still didn't respond. Maria was getting frustrated, but there was no way she was going to sit there and let him ignore her. She waited for Mr. Ford to turn to the chalkboard and start writing, and then she punched Ken on the shoulder as hard as she could.

He made a small groaning noise and turned around to look at her, scowling. Maria kept her face cool and expressionless as she thrust the note into his reluctant hand.

She watched the back of Ken's head as he unfolded and read the note. He tilted his face upward slightly, and Maria knew he was probably rolling his eyes or swearing at her under his breath, but she didn't care. Drastic times called for drastic measures, and if it took a threat to get a response out of Ken Matthews, that was just fine with her.

Hopefully he still had some desire to graduate on time. If so, the fear of flunking a required class should be enough incentive to make him show.

If not, Maria would just have to make good on her threat and tell Mr. Ford it wasn't going to work out. She couldn't spend all of her time playing therapist to Ken, especially if it wasn't going anywhere. She had more important things to work on, like finishing the project herself and completing her college essays.

And, of course, getting Conner back.

"Hey, Aames! Missed you at practice yesterday. What are you doing, blowing us off?"

Jeremy turned to see Trent, closely followed by another of their teammates, Stan Ramsey.

"Not you, man," Jeremy called back to Trent. "Just Stan." Stan sprinted up to Jeremy and pretended to wrestle with him, putting him in a headlock and throwing exaggerated punches at his head. Jeremy forced his way out of the hold and pushed Stan away.

"Take it easy, man," Jeremy said, pretending to be upset. "Do you know how long it took me to get my hair this perfect this morning?"

Trent caught up to them, chuckling. "Yeah, I can tell. It looks like you spent the better part of thirty seconds in front of the mirror, buddy," he said as they continued down the hall.

Jeremy pushed open the double doors that led to the enclosed grassy area where most of the seniors hung out during their free periods. It was nicely landscaped with shrubs and flowers, and there was even one small tree growing in the very center. Jeremy and his buddies grabbed a seat at one of the many picnic tables.

"I stopped at the vending machine and got the beverages," Trent said, distributing their usual sodas from his backpack.

"Thanks, man." Jeremy popped open his Sprite and hoped his friends wouldn't bring up his mysterious absence again.

"So, you guys comin' to the party Friday night?" Trent asked, taking a long sip from his can.

"Are you kidding?" Stan asked. "I love your parties. I wouldn't miss it for the world. Besides, Linda Ford's gonna be there, isn't she?" he asked hopefully.

"Yeah, she'll be there, but I don't know what you're getting so excited about," Trent responded, smiling. He shot a look at Jeremy, who was also grinning widely. He loved this age-old conversation. "She was at two of my parties over the summer, and you still didn't manage to ask her out."

Jeremy laughed. Stan had been talking about dating Linda since they were freshmen, but every time he was around her, he fell apart and ended up encouraging her to date whatever guy she was interested in at the time. Meanwhile she had gone through boyfriend after boyfriend, never staying with any of them too long and always breaking up with them before things got serious.

"This is it, though," Stan said. "This time I'm gonna ask her out. I can feel it." Which was, of course, what he always said. Trent and Jeremy exchanged another amused look.

"You comin', man?" Trent asked Jeremy.

"Absolutely," Jeremy responded. "I can't wait to see what you're gonna do this time."

Trent scowled at him.

"Come on, man," Jeremy continued, "you've gotta admit, something interesting always happens when you're involved."

"Interesting?" Stan jumped in. "That's an understatement." Jeremy and Stan laughed and slapped hands.

"Hey—I didn't mean to steal that cop's car," Trent said defensively.

"No. You meant to steal mine," Jeremy reminded him.

"Oh, man, that was the best!" Stan bellowed. "The look on your face when the chief of police asked you what you were doing in his Jag!" Jeremy and Stan nearly doubled over, laughing.

"How was I supposed to know? It was the same make as Jeremy's, and in the dark it looked like the same color too."

Jeremy wiped a tear from his eye. "You're just lucky that he and your dad were good friends. You could have been arrested."

"Yeah, yeah," Trent said, rolling his eyes. "Whatever."

Jeremy grinned and looked at Stan. "Trent had to mow the guy's lawn for the rest of the summer—every Saturday morning."

"Dude, do you even know how to run a lawn mower?" Stan asked, leaning forward.

"Not exactly," Trent said sheepishly. "Let's just say the chief eventually regretted his decision." He smiled. "Anyway, there won't be any car jacking this time. I'll be busy keeping Eileen happy."

Jeremy felt a pang of jealousy at Trent's wistful smile. Trent might have been unlucky with the law, but he was lucky in love.

"Cool," Jeremy said. "I bet she and Jessica will really hit it off."

"Jessica?" Stan said, belching as he crushed his empty can.

"The new girl at the coffee bar," Trent explained. "Any luck yet?"

"It could go either way at this point," Jeremy said, wondering if he had a shot at all. "I'm gonna see her this afternoon, so I should find out then."

"You should invite her to your place," Stan said, lowering one eyebrow. "You could swim in the pool, take a Jacuzzi, hang out in the sauna, play tennis. She'd be all over you."

Jeremy looked across the courtyard and gulped his soda, hoping Stan would drop the subject.

"Hey! Come to think of it, you haven't had a party at your place in a long time. What gives?"

*Oh, well,* Jeremy thought. He shifted uneasily on the bench. "I would, but I'm working so much these days that I don't have time to plan anything. It's a lot easier to just go to someone else's house. Besides, Trent's parties are the best."

"Thank you," Trent said.

"Sure, but I'd really like to show Linda your gardens. She loves that stuff."

*Oh, you mean the tangle of roots and weeds?* Jeremy thought.

"All right, I'll tell you what," he said, determined to put an end to Stan's badgering. "You ask Linda out tomorrow night, and I'll have a party at my house in the spring. Deal?"

"Deal," Stan shot back. "I'm telling you, man,

you're gonna lose that bet. I can feel it. Friday night's the night."

"I'm not holdin' my breath," Jeremy said.

"Hey! I'm totally serious!" Stan protested.

"Spring blowout at my house?" Trent teased.

As Stan and Trent started a shoving match across the table, Jeremy sighed with relief. But it was short-lived. Sure, he had dodged that bullet for a while, but how much longer could he go on lying to his friends?

"I am so dreading those skits in French class," Elizabeth said.

"Oh my God, I know." Tia giggled, her eyes wide. "Andy and I have to do ours today, and we're so not ready. We look totally pathetic. We were practicing in front of Angel last night, and he couldn't stop laughing!"

Maria sat back on her chair in the cafeteria and listened while Tia and Elizabeth exchanged scholastic tales of woe. Maria had done her skit on Monday, and she didn't feel like revisiting it.

"Conner was supposed to watch us on Tuesday afternoon, but he bailed," Tia added.

Conner. Now that was a subject Maria could talk about. Maybe she should tell Tia and Elizabeth how he gave her a ride on Monday when her car had a flat. She could see if they thought it was a good sign or not.

"You know, on Monday when—"

"Jessica and I were in the bathroom practicing ours—"

Maria let her voice trail off as Elizabeth started talking again. No one gave any sign of having heard Maria speak. Oh, well. Lunch period was almost over, and she had other things to think about—like homework. After all, since she'd likely be spending a few hours in the library alone again this afternoon, she might as well make a list of all the things she could get done.

Maria flipped open her assignment pad and noticed a big, fat blank after calculus. She'd forgotten to write down the English homework. Elizabeth was too engrossed in conversation to ask, so Maria decided to find it herself.

She grabbed Elizabeth's English notebook from the table and snapped through the pages. She'd seen Elizabeth scribble down the assignment during class, but none of the notes looked familiar.

*Oops. Wrong notebook.* Maria started to close the cover, but then something caught her eye—and her heart. Conner's name was scrawled and crossed out about twenty times on one page alone. Maria's stomach tightened.

Farther down the page, there were bits and pieces of a garbled poem—obviously something Elizabeth was working on. A lot of it had been scribbled out and written over, but a few words stood out clearly to Maria.

Love, longing, secrecy.

Maria clutched the notebook, unable to move. Elizabeth? It couldn't be.

She looked up cautiously at her friend, sure that everyone else must have noticed that the world had just come to a screeching stop—that Elizabeth would be staring at her, guilt stricken.

But she wasn't. Elizabeth was laughing it up with Tia—Conner's best friend, Tia—oblivious to Maria's insides oozing onto the floor around her.

# Andy Marsden

I saw Maria see Elizabeth's notebook.

And I saw Maria give Elizabeth this look that I've never seen before.

And I know Elizabeth is totally clueless that Maria saw anything.

I'm always noticing this kind of stuff, and being the only person who knows everything that's going on can be kind of a drag. Like I just want to make them all tell each other what's up.

But then again, it's always interesting trying to guess what's going to happen next.

# Running Interference

With every step toward the library, Maria was growing increasingly angry. She had been thinking about Elizabeth and Conner all afternoon, and she still couldn't believe it. How could Elizabeth do something like this?

*Conner is mine,* Maria thought. *I fell in love with him. I went out with him. So what if he dumped me? Isn't there some rule about this?*

Of course there was. Everyone knew that you weren't supposed to mess with your friends' exes without discussing it first. It was Dating and Friendship 101. But here was Elizabeth, crushing on Conner while Maria was still trying to work things out with him.

"And they live together!" Maria seethed aloud.

She swore under her breath as she opened the library door. To top it all off, she had a study date with a Neanderthal who wasn't even going to show. She stomped over to a table in the center of the newly refurbished library and dropped her bag. Sitting down heavily in one of the plastic molded chairs, she looked around the room. It was almost empty except for one freshman working on a computer in the corner. Even the librarian was AWOL.

*Good thing,* Maria thought. She had a feeling that even her *attitude* was too loud for the library that afternoon.

Just then the door swung open, and to Maria's surprise, Ken was standing there, scanning the room. He had his jacket on and a backpack slung over his shoulder. His tense posture told her he was ready to bolt at the slightest provocation.

He walked slowly over to the table and took a seat opposite Maria. She held her breath in an effort to keep herself from talking. She had a feeling that whatever came out of her mouth would sound belligerent.

Ken started off with his trademark blank stare, but then his brow knitted.

"What's up with you?" he asked.

"Nothing," Maria answered curtly, her words laced with anger. Where did he get off, trying to probe into *her* life?

"Excuse me for asking," Ken said.

Maria couldn't take it. It was explosion time.

"You want to know what's wrong?" she demanded, her eyes wild. "Well, allow me to enlighten you, Mr. Catatonic." Maria had so much energy, she couldn't sit still. She stood up, took a deep breath, and let herself spill.

"I just found out that Elizabeth my-so-called-best-friend Wakefield is in love with Conner McDermott, who just happens to be my boyfriend. Well, my ex-boyfriend, but that's irrelevant. Here I am trying to work things out with him, and meanwhile she's living with him and falling in love with him and not even bothering to mention it to me. Most people would have the decency to lay off a guy who their friend was dating, but not Elizabeth. No, she barges right in and tries to take him away from me. Me—her best friend! And we're talking about Elizabeth the Perfect here. Can you believe it?"

Ken just stared.

"But that's not even the worst part," Maria continued, unfazed. "I've been thinking about it all afternoon, and it finally hit me. She's been in love with him from the beginning. She's the one who tried to talk me out of dating him in the first place, acting all concerned that I'd get hurt when what she really wanted was to keep him to herself! And then when Conner dumped me, she pretended to sympathize, but she was really happy about it. I knew something didn't seem right, but I never thought Elizabeth could be such a two-faced back stabber!"

Maria noticed that the freshman boy had turned to gape at her, but she didn't care.

"You got a problem?" she snapped. The kid

immediately turned his attention back to the computer screen.

"I can't believe I didn't see it before." Maria shook her head. "I mean, she was all nervous around him at Andy's pool party, and she never wanted me to hang out with her and her new friends. God! How could I be so blind?"

Maria flopped down into her chair and let her head fall on the table. She took a few deep breaths and slowly realized she felt marginally relieved. There was something to be said for venting anger.

"Sorry," she muttered into the table.

There was no response.

Picking up her head, Maria took a peek at Ken. He was sitting there, stunned, as if someone had just slapped him across the face.

Suddenly Maria was overcome with guilt. Ken was the last person in the world equipped to deal with someone else's grief right now. He had enough of his own. She closed her eyes and winced, sitting up straight again.

"Oh God, I'm sorry, Ken. I know my screwed-up social life is the last thing you want to hear about. Who am I kidding? You don't even want to be here."

Maria stood up and grabbed her books. "I'm just going to go home and wallow."

"Wait a minute," Ken blurted out.

Maria was so startled to hear him speak, she dropped right back into her chair.

Ken shifted in his seat and cleared his throat.

"I know I'm not exactly an expert on . . . relationships, but I think that if Liz liking Conner bothers you so much, you should just tell her," Ken said.

Maria looked over her shoulder to see if she was being filmed for some kind of gag. Ken was dispensing advice?

"I mean, I haven't been hanging out with her lately or anything," Ken continued, sitting up slightly as if talking was boosting his strength, "but I always kind of thought she was the direct-approach type."

Ken held Maria's gaze for only a moment before he looked down and scratched the back of his neck with one hand.

"Thanks," she said, feeling strangely warmed by his words. Ken just shrugged and flipped open his notebook as though he might actually be planning to do some work.

Maria sat watching him for a moment, not sure which surprised her more: the fact that Ken was actually making sense or the knowledge that he had just spoken more than two sentences in a row.

Will froze when he walked through the door at House of Java. He had come to meet up with Melissa and some friends after football practice, but the last person he had expected to see was Jessica Wakefield.

She was behind the counter, pouring coffee, serving biscotti from a big glass, and looking totally beautiful. Since when did she work here?

"Hey, buddy! Get outta the way!"

"What?" Will said, glancing behind him.

"You're blocking the door," a scrawny kid said.

"Oh, sorry," Will answered, stepping aside. He could have flattened the kid with his left pinky, but there was no point. At least the guy had startled Will out of his gaping stupor.

A couple of underclassmen at a table near the door giggled in his direction, and he felt his face redden. But it didn't matter as long as Jessica hadn't caught him acting like a fool.

Will shot her a nervous glance, but she was just going about her business as if she hadn't seen him.

*Did she really not see me, or is she ignoring me?* Will wondered.

A quick look at the clock revealed that he had some time before Melissa arrived. Maybe he should try to talk to Jessica again. Every time he'd approached her in the last few weeks, she'd bolted, but she couldn't run away if she was working.

Will walked up to the counter and joined the line. His heart was slamming against his chest— as he waited for her to see him, wondering what she'd say, if she'd say anything. He couldn't stand watching her and agonizing over when she'd look up, so he turned his back to the counter, pretending to be searching the room for someone.

*Should I just order?* Will wondered. *Should I ask*

*her to talk to me? Ask her to take a break?* The line inched forward, and the girl two places in front of him started to order. He heard Jessica laugh, and then he chickened out. He stepped back from the line—just in time.

The bells over the door jangled and Will, sweating from his near encounter, saw Melissa walk in with a few of her friends from the cheerleading squad.

"Hi, Will," Melissa said loudly, giving him a big hug and kissing him lightly.

Jessica glanced up, saw Melissa, and looked away quickly, turning her back to the line as she busied herself behind the counter.

Will's heart constricted as he watched Jessica's shaky hands. He knew she was nervous around Melissa, and she was probably sickened by the sight of his face.

The tall blond guy who was working behind the counter touched Jessica's shoulder.

"Hey, Jessica, could you go in the back and grab a box of straws?" he asked.

Will's stomach turned as Melissa looked up at the sound of Jessica's name.

"That's Jessica?" she said.

"I thought her sister worked here," Cherie said, narrowing her eyes as Jessica disappeared into the back room.

Lila was standing on her toes to see over the

131

line at the counter. "Nope, that was her," Lila said. "Maybe she and Liz couldn't stand being away from each other, so they decided to work together."

"Oh, how sweet," Melissa drawled.

Melissa stepped toward the line with a slight smile on her face, undoubtedly scripting some veiled insult for Jessica's return.

"C'mon. Let's grab a table," Will said, reaching for her hand.

Melissa was about to protest, but Will tugged her arm firmly and she followed without a fight. The others fell in step behind them. Will was beginning to wonder how Melissa's friends managed to get to school every day without Melissa to lead them.

As they walked toward the back corner, Lila offered to get everyone's coffee, and Will breathed a sigh of relief. He had planned to do it himself to keep Melissa away from the counter. But then he would have had to spend the rest of the night reassuring Melissa that he hadn't just gone up there to talk to Jessica.

Will tried to tune in as Melissa and her friends started to discuss their plans for the upcoming weekend. But he had to concentrate so hard on *not* looking at Jessica, he could barely even hear himself think. He had only one requirement for their weekend plans anyway—he didn't want to run into Jessica again. He was tired of running interference.

When Jeremy walked into House of Java, there was no line at the counter. *No excuses,* Jeremy thought. *Just get it over with.*

Jeremy took a deep breath and plastered a confident grin on his face. As he approached, Jessica looked up and smiled. A good sign. Now if he could just keep his palms from sweating and sticking to the poster he had rolled up behind his back . . .

"Why do I feel like you're about to spring something on me?" Jessica asked, her eyes narrowed.

"Probably because I am," Jeremy said. "Prepare to be awed by my artistic talent." Jeremy pulled the poster board out and laid it flat on the counter in front of Jessica.

She studied the collage for a moment, and then her face drained of color.

"What is this?" she said weakly, without taking her eyes off the poster.

"What do you think it is?" Jeremy said playfully, trying to gauge her reaction.

Jessica lifted her head slowly, tentatively.

"Well, it looks like my drama project, but—"

"I did it last night when I got home," Jeremy jumped in. "Do you like it?"

"I . . . I—"

Tears. Oh, no. Jeremy couldn't believe it. She was going to cry.

"Oh God. I'm sorry, Jess," Jeremy said. "Don't cry. I just figured since it was giving you so much trouble—"

"No. It's okay." Jessica swallowed hard and looked up at him again. Her eyes were shining with unshed tears, but she was smiling. "Don't be sorry. It's—is this really how you see me?"

"Yeah," Jeremy said, his voice barely above a whisper. "I think you're pretty amazing, actually."

A single tear ran down Jessica's cheek. Jeremy pulled a napkin out of the counter dispenser and handed it to her.

"Thanks," Jessica said, dabbing at her cheek. "I don't know what's wrong with me." She quickly blew her nose. "So, when are you picking me up for that party?" she asked.

Jeremy's heart skipped a beat, and he took a quick breath before answering. "How does eight o'clock sound?" he asked, managing to keep the hyper-excitement out of his voice.

"Tomorrow at eight," Jessica said. She picked up the collage gingerly as if it were a true work of art. "That sounds perfect."

*Perfect*, Jeremy repeated to himself. It was amazing, but even after everything that had happened this week, it was turning out to be just that.

Perfect.

# Ken Matthews

## AP History Project: Part One

The road to women's suffrage began in 1848 at the Seneca Falls Convention in New York, where Elizabeth Cady Stanton, Lucretia Mott, Susan B. Anthony, and—

Who cares about this crap anyway? Women won the right to vote. Period. End of story.

I'm so sick of dissecting everything and analyzing the hell out of it. That's what people keep doing to me. They probe and prod and try to say all the right things so I'll spill my guts and "let the healing begin." Either that or they just avoid me altogether like I might be contagious or something.

But with Maria today, it was different. For once I wasn't the one with the problem—and it felt good. Maybe I'm a jerk because I kind of enjoyed seeing someone else in pain for a change, but I don't care. I just know that when Maria started bitching about Elizabeth, it was the first time in a long time that I'd felt something other than pity from another person.

I still don't give a damn about this freakin' history project, but at least for a minute this afternoon, I didn't feel like some charity case.

# Jessica Wakefield

<u>Absolutely</u> <u>Amazing</u> <u>Things</u> <u>That</u> <u>Have</u> <u>Happened</u>
<u>to</u> <u>Me</u> <u>Lately</u> <u>That</u> <u>I</u> <u>Didn't</u> <u>Mess</u> <u>Up</u>

1. Jeremy did my drama project for me. Key terms used in project: "The Most Beautiful Girl in the World," "Isn't She Lovely?" and "The Eyes Have It."

2. Jeremy asked me out again. Thankfully, I said yes this time, and we're going out on Friday night. (Unfortunately I don't even begin to live up to his expectations, and he's sure to dump me as soon as he figures that out. Probably about fifteen minutes into the date.)

# CHAPTER

## An Emotional Noose

**9**

"Elizabeth! Are you all right?" Andy whispered, leaning across the aisle in creative writing.

"Never better," Elizabeth hissed, clamping her hand down on her knee to stop her leg from bouncing. Her eyes darted to the clock for about the eightieth time in the last forty minutes. Was it possible? Could she actually make it out of here without being called on?

"You're next," Andy whispered.

"I know," she said through clenched teeth. Mr. Quigley was calling students in alphabetical order. Julie Voss was walking up there now. But maybe she'd written an epic poem or a short story or something that would take a while for her to read.

Elizabeth risked a glance back at Conner. He smiled slightly and nodded. Then he mouthed the words "can't wait." So much for hoping he'd forgotten about their laundry-room conversation.

"Right," Elizabeth muttered, facing forward

again. "Rattle off some lousy song lyrics, call it a work in progress, and the whole room swoons."

"What?" Andy whispered.

"Mr. Marsden, Ms. Wakefield. Please give your classmates some respect," Mr. Quigley called out.

Great. Elizabeth's cheek shade deepened.

Why, oh why had she told Conner he might be surprised by what she'd written? *Wait and see,* her mind mimicked. He had to know she'd been working on it for a while. What if it stank? What if he laughed? What if they all laughed?

Elizabeth sat up straight, trying to at least give the appearance of calm. There was no more time for agonizing. This was it. Julie Voss was walking back to her seat.

"Thank you, Julie," Mr. Quigley said in the same authoritative tone with which he had thanked every other student who had read so far. He might have loved what she had written or he might have thought it was complete crap, but the voice still would have been the same.

He looked down at his grade book, trailing his finger down the column of names on the left-hand side. Then he looked up and turned to Elizabeth.

"Ms. Wakefield," he said evenly. Elizabeth automatically rose and walked to the front of the room. She could feel herself trembling and just hoped that the paper wouldn't shake in her hands while she read. This was crazy. She was usually so at ease speaking in public, and she always aced oral presentations.

Before she started reading, she glanced at Conner one last time. He looked back and gave her a hokey thumbs-up, which was clearly meant in jest. Elizabeth tucked her chin and stared down at the page. How could she possibly go through with this?

"This is called 'Your Silence,'" Elizabeth said. She cleared her throat, said a little prayer, and began.

> *I sit in your silence, scared.*
> *Waiting patiently for recognition.*
>
> *For a word.*
> *For a breath.*
> *For a touch.*
>
> *But I am raw.*
>
> *Because I watch your hands instead*
> *of writing*
> *and listen for your breath instead*
> *of breathing.*
>
> *It's strange,*
> *how close to you I feel*

*and the need I have*
*to help you,*
*to make you smile.*

*And yet I'm still sitting here,*
*waiting,*
*for you to let me in.*

As Elizabeth finished, she heard the paper fluttering in her hand and grabbed her wrist to stop it from shaking. The room was silent. She looked up, hyperaware that she wasn't the only one in the room holding her breath.

She risked a glance at Conner. The smirk was gone. The mocking grin was gone. He was just staring at her. Openly, blatantly staring at her.

And then the bell rang.

Maria had been avoiding Elizabeth all day, and it hadn't been easy. Especially considering they had homeroom and three morning classes together. There had been a lot of sitting near doors and sprinting the moment the bell rang.

But next period was French class, and it was going to be tough. Maria always sat in a cluster with Elizabeth, Jessica, Tia, and Andy. What was she supposed to do—diss everyone and sit with Melissa Fox or something? No, thank you.

Maria stepped back from her locker, slammed

the door shut, and jumped slightly in surprise. Ken was standing right next to her.

"Hey," he said, burrowing his hands into his pockets.

"Hey, Ken," she said, still self-conscious about her tirade in the library.

"Have you talked to Elizabeth yet?" he asked, his voice low.

"Um . . . no," Maria said. She was surprised by his seeming concern.

"Oh." Disappointment. What was going on here? Was Ken trying to . . . become involved in the world of the living? He leaned back against the locker and stared across the hall.

"I guess I've kind of been avoiding her." Maria looked sideways at Ken, waiting for some kind of reaction. Maybe he'd tell her that talking to Elizabeth would actually be a bad idea and that it would all blow over.

"Well, you can't avoid her forever," Ken said, eyeing her briefly. "Keeping it inside is only going to make things worse." He kicked at the floor with the toe of his battered work boot. "Consider the source."

Maria turned slowly and leaned back next to him, pondering what she might or might not be able to say.

"You know, you just came dangerously close to opening up," she said cautiously.

Ken let out a half snort, half laugh. "Yeah, well, don't get used to it."

Maria laughed and saw Ken smile out of the corner of her eye. It felt good to pull that out of him.

"Okay. I'll talk to Liz right after school and find out what's going on," Maria said, pushing away from the locker.

Ken stood up straight. "Well. Where's Liz now?" he asked.

"What, now you're gonna give me 'there's no time like the present'?" Maria asked incredulously.

"Better you than me," Ken said with a shrug.

Maria sighed. The sheer fact that Ken was taking such an interest made her feel obligated to act on his suggestion.

"She should be getting out of Quigley's class," she said. She narrowed her eyes at him, but Ken just stared back, unflinching.

"All right. Fine," she said. "But you're coming with me." She reached out and grabbed ahold of Ken's dingy denim sleeve, pulling him down the hall toward Elizabeth's creative-writing classroom.

She just hoped Conner was long gone by the time she got there. There was no way she could handle them both at once.

Elizabeth walked out of class with her stomach in knots, but feeling relieved and somehow exhilarated after reading her poem. The other students in her class were filing out too, and the absence of normal postclass chatter was obvious. Clearly her poem had gotten their attention.

Just then she felt a heavy hand on her shoulder. Elizabeth's heart skipped a beat, and she held her breath as she turned around.

It was Conner. And for once the sarcastic shield that usually masked his face was gone, leaving an open vulnerability Elizabeth had never seen before.

"What was that all about?" he asked, looking her directly in the eye.

"What was what all about?" she answered. She was stalling for time—trying to figure out what he was thinking.

"Oh, come on," he said, leaning in closer to her, a bit of the bite back. "Your poem. It was about me."

Elizabeth looked at him, her eyes wide. She could play too. "What makes you say that?" she asked innocently.

Conner smirked, his eyes dancing.

"All right, then," he said, lifting his chin. "I dare you to read it again. To my face this time."

Elizabeth's heart began to pound in her ears. She and Conner locked eyes, and suddenly the rest of the world was a muted haze. She was dimly aware of the buzz of other students in the hallway, but she was determined to hold Conner's gaze. It was a standoff, and Elizabeth wasn't going to be the first to look away.

In fact, she was going to make sure of it.

"I sit in your silence, scared," Elizabeth recited, her voice just above a whisper. "Waiting . . . patiently for recognition."

Conner smiled and closed his eyes, obviously surprised at her audacity. When he opened them again, Elizabeth was right there waiting, gazing directly into his eyes.

"For a word," she said, smiling. "For a breath. For a—"

She stopped, catching her breath in her throat. Her heart was pounding so loudly, he had to hear it. Especially since he was hovering ever closer.

"For a—"

"Touch?" Conner said in his throaty whisper. He raised his hand to her cheek, and Elizabeth closed her eyes. His fingers grazed her skin, and she felt him moving closer. Felt his breath on her face.

"Touch," Elizabeth whispered.

She felt his lips an instant before they brushed her own. He kissed her. Gently at first, and then harder, with more certainty. He slid his hand beneath her hair and pulled her closer, cupping the back of her head with his palm.

Elizabeth was vaguely aware that all of her books had dropped to the floor, but she didn't care because as she gripped Conner's arms with her shaking fingers, she felt certain it must be a dream.

\* \* \*

"I know you're right. I need to talk to her," Maria said for the fourth time, as if saying it over and over would help her believe it. Still, as she and Ken made their way toward Mr. Quigley's room, Maria had a sinking sense that now wasn't the time for a confrontation.

"Hey, there she is," Ken said, giving Maria a nudge in the right direction. Maria wiped her hands against her thighs and started to walk toward Elizabeth. She still had no idea what she was going to say, but she had to try. She had to get it over with.

But just as Maria was about to call out Elizabeth's name, the crowded hall cleared slightly and she got a good view of her friend . . . and of whom she was standing with.

Maria stopped short. Impulsively she grabbed Ken's arm and clung to it.

It was Conner. And he was standing a little too close to Elizabeth. Way too close.

"What's wrong?" Ken asked.

"Look at them," Maria said quietly.

Ken obliged. "Yeah?"

"What are you, blind? They look like they just kissed or something. They're all red!" Maria hissed. She swallowed back a disgusted lump that was rapidly forming in her throat. "And they're all smiley."

It looked like they were sharing some kind of private joke. Maybe some kind of private joke about what an oblivious loser Maria was. Conner bent down

146

to pick up a book, and when he passed it to Elizabeth, she giggled with a little too much enthusiasm.

"Ugh. I'm gonna be sick," Maria said, holding her stomach with her free hand. She turned away and started back down the hall. Ken lost his balance as she pulled him with her.

"What?" he asked, falling into step. "She dropped her book. He picked it up. What's the big deal?"

Maria ducked around a corner and leaned against the cool, cinder-block wall. She fought back tears. "You don't get it, Ken. This is all wrong. Liz and Conner aren't even supposed to like each other." She felt tears spring to her eyes. "I was trying to get them together. So they could be friends. So we could all—so we could all—"

She reached up and wiped both eyes with her hands.

"Maria, calm down," Ken said, looking not a little bit scared. "You didn't see anything just now."

Maria blinked up at Ken. Maybe he was right. He was, after all, an impartial observer, and Maria was tied to the situation with an emotional noose.

But the way Conner was looking at her . . . Was it possible that they were seeing each other behind Maria's back? No. Elizabeth would never do that. But something was going on. Something.

And Maria had to find out what it was.

# Elizabeth Wakefield

Now _that_ was worth agonizing over.

# Conner McDermott

I know when I'm beaten.

# CHAPTER 10
## The Big Date

Jeremy watched as Jessica crossed the large foyer of Trent's house, smiling shyly as she maneuvered through the small clusters of people. Almost everyone in the room turned to look as she passed by.

"Did you find it okay?" Jeremy asked when Jessica was back by his side.

"The bathroom?" she asked, smoothing the front of her white dress. "I think I found four of them."

Jeremy laughed. "The pitfalls of having a big house. You can never decide which bathroom to use."

"Yeah, I guess," Jessica said distractedly. Her eyes darted around the room as if she were expecting to see someone she didn't want to see.

"Are you all right?" Jeremy asked. Jessica looked up at him, but before she could answer, Trent came over and slung his arms over their shoulders.

"Everybody here has one question," he said, looking back and forth between the two of them.

"What is the hottest girl in the room doing with this guy?"

He slapped Jeremy on the chest as Jessica blushed.

"He's right, you know," Jeremy said. "It doesn't make any sense."

"You have no idea," Jessica said under her breath, tucking her hair behind her ears.

Jeremy's brow knitted. "What do you mean?"

"Oh, nothing," Jessica said, smiling.

"Hey, guys! Is this the famous Jessica Wakefield?" Stan walked over and offered Jessica a cup of soda.

"Jessica, this is Stan," Jeremy said as Jessica accepted the drink. He couldn't help noticing that Stan looked unusually coiffed. His short hair was gelled, his shirt was tucked, and he wasn't bleeding, so he'd obviously spent some extra time shaving. "And he's oddly clean," Jeremy added.

"And he's oddly without Linda," Trent said, raising an eyebrow.

"Who's Linda?" Jessica asked.

"Well—," Jeremy and Trent began in unison.

Stan held up a hand. "Let me tell her myself," he said. "Maybe Jessica can give me a woman's opinion. Come on, Jess. Let's talk." Stan tilted his head in the direction of the parlor, where Linda was probably hanging with her friends. Knowing Stan, Jeremy thought Stan probably wanted Linda to see him with Jessica in some vain attempt to make her jealous.

"Um . . . okay," Jessica said, shooting a confused smile at Jeremy and Trent.

"Don't worry about the big guy," Jeremy said. "He's harmless."

"Damn, she is beautiful," Trent said once Jessica was safely out of earshot. "I'm not kidding, man. Every guy in the room wants her."

Jeremy took a sip of his soda and smiled. "Well, they can't have her," he said. "I've put in too much work already."

Up until tonight anyway. So far, the date itself had been effortless. There hadn't been any sudden emergencies at home to make him late, he had scrounged up five dollars so he could pay for gas, and Jessica was obviously a little bit nervous, but she was warming up quickly. The only thing that had thrown Jeremy had been the scope of her house—no—mansion. From the size of the palace she lived in, she was used to everything first-class. He just hoped he was right about her and that she wouldn't care once she found out about his new, lower tax bracket.

*Unless I keep it a secret from her too,* Jeremy thought. Even thinking about his secrecy brought him down momentarily, but Jeremy pushed the heaviness away. He was here to have fun.

"Well, he's dancing with her!" Jessica announced

happily, breaking him out of his thoughts.

"What?" Jeremy glanced at Trent, and they both peeked into the parlor. Sure enough, Stan was holding Linda in his arms, swaying slowly to a soft ballad.

Jeremy looked at Jessica, stunned. "How did you do that?"

Jessica grinned. "It's a talent."

"You're amazing," he said, causing her cheeks to redden adorably. It just made his heart beat faster. He was constantly astounded by her sweetness, her kindness, and everything else about her. Jeremy was simply in awe.

"Do you want to dance?" Jeremy asked, gazing into her deep blue-green eyes.

"Sure," Jessica answered.

"That's my cue," Trent said before he disappeared into the crowd. But Jeremy didn't even see his friend leave.

"Okay. I know that Kyle invited us to this party, but whose house are we at again?" Cherie asked, tugging at the hemline of her little black dress while she, Gina, Melissa, and Will waited on the front porch of a large, old house in Big Mesa.

"I told you in the car," Gina said, obviously irritated.

Will stood uncomfortably behind the three girls, hoping someone would answer the door soon. Melissa's friends were in *über*bitch mode. They'd spent fifteen minutes arguing over whose car to take, another fifteen over whether Cherie should change her dress because the three of them were all wearing black, and another fifteen fixing their makeup while he left the car idling in the driveway. Will needed to be around some testosterone—now.

"What is this guy's name? Troy? Trey?" Melissa asked, leaning on the bell again.

"It's Trent," Will said, not bothering to keep the bite from his voice. "Kyle plays on the football team with him at Big Mesa, and Trent told everyone to invite friends. Supposedly he throws great parties."

"Thank you, Will," Melissa said exaggeratedly, obviously responding to his less than patient tone.

Luckily the door opened and a tall, blond guy ushered them inside.

"Come on in. Trent's around here somewhere," the guy said.

"Thanks," Will answered as he and the three girls walked into the large foyer. There was a huge winding staircase surrounded by partyers, and people were walking in and out of two adjacent rooms. "Nice place," Will said, looking around for some of the El Carro guys who were supposed to be there.

"Seriously," Melissa said, her eyes wide. Will

knew she was taking in all the expensive clothes and determining whether her own measured up.

"Hey! There's Kyle," he said, spotting a group of friends across the room. It was time for Melissa to listen to some guy talk for a change. He gently took Melissa's arm and steered her toward his friends. But Melissa was rooted to the spot. Something else had caught her attention, and Will turned to see what it was. But all he had to see was the look on Melissa's face to know.

Jessica.

Will felt his brow start to sweat as he frantically searched the room. When he found her, he couldn't believe his eyes. She was standing with Jeremy Aames, the captain of Big Mesa's football team, and she was laughing. Carefree and gorgeous, she looked just like she had the day he first met her.

She looked happy.

And Melissa was on the move.

By the time Will snapped out of his stupor, Melissa, Gina, and Cherie were already closing in on Jessica. She hadn't seen them yet, and Will had to stop them before she did.

"Melissa, no!" Will called out. Melissa flinched, but didn't stop. Will lurched forward and grabbed her elbow. She whirled around and flung his hand away.

"Ow! Will! What are you doing?" Melissa spat.

"Not here, Melissa," Will said, searching her

face for a trace of the goodness he knew she had somewhere inside. "Don't do this."

Something seemed to break inside Melissa, and she lowered her eyes. Her rigid body relaxed, and she looked up at Will, an apology in her eyes. Will held his breath. Had he finally gotten to her? Was she finally going to stop?

"Gee, I wonder who invited the slut." Cherie's voice carried over the music. It was too late. Will watched, riveted in horror as Jessica whipped around.

"Cherie," she said. Her face was a mask of pain and fear.

"Melissa, do something," Will whispered. "This isn't the place."

"What do you expect me to do, Will?" Melissa asked, tears in her eyes.

"Stop them. Call off your attack dogs—"

"Save your little girlfriend?" Melissa asked, her voice growing hard. "That's what you really want, isn't it?"

Will didn't respond.

"What's wrong, Jessica?" Gina said, her voice cold and mocking. "Did you have to start scrounging for dates at Big Mesa now that you've worked your way through all of the Sweet Valley guys?" Gina and Cherie laughed wickedly as Jessica stared at them, stunned into silence. A few people turned to gape, and Jessica's eyes scanned the room as if she were looking for a friend.

Will grabbed both of Melissa's wrists and held them together. "I swear if you don't go over there right now, I'm outta here."

Melissa stared into his eyes defiantly. Then she wrested herself free, turned her back on him, and didn't move a muscle. Will found himself staring at the tiled floor, struggling to contain his temper.

When he finally looked up again, Jessica was gone and Melissa hadn't moved. He knew she was waiting for him to say something. But he had nothing to say.

As Will walked out of the party, he was certain of one thing. There would be no more wussing out. It was time to leave this relationship for good.

"Who the hell do you think you are?" Jeremy snapped, stepping forward and putting himself between Jessica and the psychotic girls who were attacking her.

"We're just friends of Jessica's from Sweet Valley," the redhead said, smiling innocently. "And who are you? The boyfriend of the hour?"

Jeremy crossed his arms in front of his chest. "Why don't you and your sidekicks get the hell out of here?"

"Who died and left you in charge?" girl number two asked snottily.

"I'm in charge," Trent said, walking into the room with Joe Datolli, who had obviously run to find him when the whole thing started. "And I'm telling you to leave."

The color drained from the redhead's face, leaving her freckles in high relief. "Fine. We don't need your loser party anyway."

For a moment Jeremy couldn't move. He was too stunned that anyone could actually be that cruel. And especially to someone as sweet and vulnerable as Jessica.

Jessica.

Jeremy turned around to see if she was okay, but she was gone.

"Where's Jess?" he asked no one in particular.

"She ducked out," Trent said. "She looked pretty upset."

"Maybe she went to the bathroom," Stan offered.

"Yeah. Do you want me to go look for her?" Linda asked.

Jeremy looked around the room helplessly. "No, that's okay. I'll find her." He glanced at his friends' stricken faces. "Just do me a favor. Find out who invited those girls and pummel whoever it is, all right?"

"My pleasure," Stan said.

Jeremy searched the kitchen, parlor, and living room, then knocked on all the bathroom doors, but Jessica was nowhere to be found. He ran back through the foyer and out the front door. There were dozens of cars parked in the driveway and on the street, and a few party stragglers were walking across the huge front lawn.

Jeremy squinted and scanned the grounds. He spotted a shadow at the edge of the yard. It was dark, but he was pretty sure the shadow was Jessica.

He opened his mouth to shout to her, but then a familiar car screeched to a stop in front of the house.

"Mom?" Jeremy said.

Jeremy's mother jumped out of the driver's seat and ran across the lawn toward the house. She was wearing a suit, and she moved awkwardly. Something was wrong. He'd never seen his mother run like that before.

Then he saw her face, and his heart stopped. Mascara streaked down her colorless cheeks, and her hair was stuck to her face in matted wisps. When she reached him, she collapsed into his arms, sobbing, and Jeremy knew what had happened before she even spoke the words.

"Jeremy. It's your father. He's had a heart attack."

# MARIA SLATER

## 4:11 P.M.

### *The Case against Elizabeth*

1. When I first mentioned I thought Conner was cute, Elizabeth tried every argument imaginable to turn me off.

2. When she found out I hooked up with him, she bolted from my car with serious high drama. (Amazing how everything takes on a new meaning in retrospect. I remember thinking all the smoke at the Riot had made her sick to her stomach.)

3. While Conner and I were together, she kept trying to convince me he wasn't *really* interested. Maybe he wasn't, but still.

4. The poem.

5. I don't even believe I'm going to write this, but I saw what I saw. And when I saw Conner and Elizabeth in the hall, they definitely looked like two people in love.

I can't believe Conner kissed me right there in the hall. I wish Jessica had been there to see it. She would have freaked and told me how disgusting he is, but inside she would have been proud of her prude sister.

I wonder what Tia would have done if she'd seen us. Or Andy. Or Enid. Or Megan. Or (I'm so evil) Todd.

Ugh!

I wish I could just call Tia and tell her about it, but I can't. Because this is Conner. And I have a feeling I shouldn't say anything to our friends until I figure out what's <u>really</u> going on between us. I have to play it safe because I don't want to mess things up. This is too important.

But why couldn't one of my friends have just been there so I had someone to talk to about this? I'd take anyone!

Well, anyone except Maria, of course.

# JESSICA WAKEFIELD
## 11:55 P.M.

My life is ruined. There's no way I can deal with Jeremy looking at me that way. The way all the kids at school look at me. The way he has to look at me now that he knows what a loser I am.

# JEREMY AAMES

## 1:16 A.M.

So much for the perfect-family act.
The play is over. The curtain is drawn.
What do they call this in dramatic
terms? Divine intervention?

.

Check out the **all-new....**

**Sweet Valley Web site—**

# www.sweetvalley.com

# New Features

## Cool Prizes

The
**ONLY**
official
Web site!

## Hot Links

And much more!

Bantam

BFYR 202

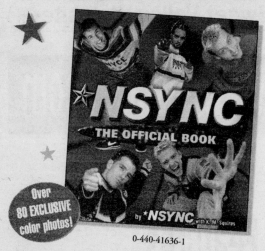